Dear Nassir,

Enjoy !

SIX DEVILS IN THE
SAN FERNANDO VALLEY

Always look for the Angels!

E. Mennie

Published by Opus Coast Publishing

Copyright © 2014 Ernie Mannix

ISBN 978-0-9914067-0-8

First Edition, 2014

Cover Art: Damonza

For Mr. and Mrs. Ernest Mannix Sr.

SIX DEVILS IN THE
SAN FERNANDO VALLEY

ERNIE MANNIX

ACKNOWLEDGMENTS

1. Engelhardt, Zephyrin 1851-1934. Missions and Missionaries of California. San Francisco: James H. Barry, 1915. Print.
2. Shuck, Oscar Tully. *The California Scrap Book.* California: H.H Bancroft, 1869. Print.

This novel would not have been possible without the support of my wife and wonderful children. Thanks also to Sara Anne Fox and Bryon Quertermous.

A very special thanks to this novel's archangel, Michael McGruther, for his insight, encouragement and vision.

PROLOGUE

"We saw a very pleasant and spacious valley. We descended to it and stopped close to a watering place, which is a large pool. Near it we found a village of heathen, very friendly and docile. We gave to this plain the name of Santa Catalina de Bononia de Los Encinos. It has on its hills and its valleys many live oak and walnuts.

– Father Juan Crespi, 1769" (1).

*

A GREAT VALLEY, HOME to the ancient people of what was to be the state of California, came to be civilized by Father Juan Crespi and his Spanish expedition. Along with Junipero Serra, Father Crespi set about California finally finding his way south over the mountains into a vast dry wilderness where he established his outpost, and turned this valley's primitive heathen to a waiting Christ. The natives were gathered to his mission at San Fernando, a new home for civility and its requested laborers, and as Spain had decreed, a much needed portal to God.

Eventually, followers built homes close by, etching friendly delineating paths in between their respective lands. They grew crops to sustain themselves and traded them, up and up, advancing themselves into the hierarchy of new communities. Irrigation was key to growth, so as time burned on, the water baptized new large ranches, expansive green orchards and growing towns. The hot dry grass below the hellish hot hills was tamed into ranches that grew away from the mission, with land parceled to families, some large with grand, sustainable names.

Years later, the post war boom of the promising paradise, was sewn large by smaller forgettable names, whose many children became failed actors and actresses, coming, going, living and dying amongst the growing streets, while ghosts appearing and disappearing in the decaying street cars, faded away in the dozing of the former great estates, making way for the burdening squeeze of foul apartments, crowding, pollution and profiting cemeteries.

The grand families living on in their street's names alone, Lankershim, Burbank and Chandler, burning hot in the summer sun, flooded in the February rains, and roped off by police, when the valley's gangs, so far away from the influence of a long forgotten Father Crespi, drip human blood down into their cracks.

From a bird's eye view, high above the Ventura Freeway, a slow moving pickup truck is in the right lane, tossing blue smoke, being cursed at, horned at—piled high with old mattresses. Moving on down, not minding the smoke, we see the handsome brown-skinned driver, clear-eyed, smiling—and just going about his business.

CHAPTER 1

THE WATER TOWER

I RECEIVED A NOTICE from my landlord, asking me to vacate in sixty days. The letter said that I've been behind in my rent too many times, and there were too many people waiting for apartments. It was a handwritten note, which for this town was a very old-fashioned touch.

Having been recently fired from my job of four years, I realized that I had finally become one of *those* people—an LA casualty. No love, little money, behind in my rent, no job, and worst of all, in this town of enormous dreams, I had no hope. My job wasn't a dream job, but it was a living, doing rewrites for the big studio up the street.

There was a news story on television about the recent heavy rains, causing the Los Angeles River to swell and run unusually fast. Rain at this time of the year is odd, and I really wanted to see this force of nature—I wanted to see the churning, cemented urban river at its mightiest. On my drive down Lankershim Boulevard, the heavy rain came to an end, and the sun came out. I continued on, hoping that the river would still be at its full potential. I longed to see some roaring rapids. I wanted a wild show.

Driving along the boulevard, I noticed some nasty car exhaust smoke hanging in the air. It grew thicker and thicker as I got closer and closer to its source. It turned out to be one of those old pickup trucks—those strange ones that carry mattresses piled up in the rear. At the light I pulled alongside the smoke-belching gross polluter, when suddenly its large, menacing driver looked over at me and scowled. I immediately realized that I'd forgotten a rule—in Los Angeles, you don't lock eyes at traffic lights—there's no upside to it.

I arrived at the river and was pleased to see that the local news hadn't made too much of it. Usually, they'd hype even the smallest puddle after a rainstorm, but this storm warranted their attention, for the river was fast and deep, with treacherous fallen tree branches and odd garbage racing by. I saw what looked like pages from a discarded script floating past, possibly thrown in by a frustrated writer somewhere upriver.

I guess that's when I realized the real reason for my visit—I'd had enough. I was done.

I turned to look at the bright rays that emerged from behind the storm clouds, when all at once it hit me; the sun was the creator of the California myth, and the single most popular attraction in the state. Constant sunshine and great weather, silly people often confuse it with happiness.

The sun never took away my pain or gave me back my good life, lost loves, or plagiarized scripts. It could never restore the years of wasted toil, or bring me the biggest prize I'd given up; a normal family life—one that would let me hear the words "I love you," from a wife or a child.

They wanted me out in sixty days? I figured they'd find me before then.

Shooting myself was out of the question. Too messy, and then there'd be all the police photos of the gruesome scene. I didn't want those to be my legacy.

The river will do it for me—all I need to do is relax, I thought to myself.

I lifted my right foot forward and began to take my last steps toward the fast tumultuous water. To deepen my denial, I kept my eyes on the blinding, intense sunlight and stepped closer to the edge. The large sand pebbles at the cemented rim, acted like a lubricant and slipped my foot forward. They crunched under my boots and served as the final warning of what was sure to be remembered as a sad life. In my religion, suicide is considered a sin, and although I was trying to ignore it, I knew that I would soon pay for this crime against my soul.

All at once, like an explosion, he came out of nowhere and deftly wrapped his large arms around my waist aggressively pulling me back from the river.

Having been prepared to go through with it, my coursing adrenaline pumped up the shock and surprise of his forceful grip, very nearly arresting my heart.

"It's a sin you know," he said, somewhat winded—his large face filled with a pitiful anger. "You of all people should know—it's a sin."

I stood there astonished, for facing me was a very large olive-skinned man, his massive sweaty chest heaving with breath. The only thing that stopped me fleeing from this aggressive giant, were his scolding words—muggers don't scold.

"Why did you stop me?" I caught my breath then added, "Hey, who the hell are you?"

"You know why I stopped you, amigo. You know what you were about to do."

We stood there staring at each other for about five or ten seconds, though in my highly excited state it felt like several hours. When my adrenaline drained down I came to recognize him as the driver of the old pickup truck—the one piled high with mattresses.

"Why are you following me?" I said. "I see you and that damned pickup truck everywhere."

The large man looked at me, and was not pleased.

"Hey, amigo, don't be a hater man, not all brown fellows driving pickups loaded with mattresses look alike!"

Then after a frightening uncomfortable silence, he broke the ice with a big belly laugh. The timbre of the laugh was deep and warm. He was truly a giant of a man.

"My name is Roberto—we have to talk."

*

(The following is an incident that happened two years ago. It's based on an interview by Detective Vega LAPD, and inserted here for continuity.)

A car door opens in the guest parking lot of the very famous San Fernando Valley movie studio. Two eighteen year old cousins get out of the car, adjusting their blouses, touching loose bracelets, flipping their hair.

Ron Carson, their widowed uncle and father, looks tired and careworn, the burden of sole parenthood airing minuscule complaints through subtle body language. He glances up slowly at the studio's water tower, which proudly declares that he and his charges have finally arrived at their important destination.

The years of dance, drama lessons and countless star-worshipping magazine subscriptions have finally brought this genetically bound trio here, past the tower's watchful eye, and into the historic movie studio for an appointment with the top man.

Dad's dress is neat, though bland and unfashionable. The girls, Janice and Courtney Carson, look much older than their years and project a palpable provocative attitude. One could sense the man's apprehension and quiet disapproval, his partly down-turned mouth hinting at a disdain for the society that coerced him into believing that the girls were behaving and dressing acceptably.

"I'll walk you as far as the office, okay girls? I want you both to be careful today. Do you have enough money?"

The doting father and careful uncle isn't given the chance to proudly lead his girls along, for they are eager to make their appointment time and begin to move at a brisk pace. Ron starts to fall behind as they move deeper and deeper into the vast old movie studio. He tries to catch up to them, pretending to himself that they actually want him by their side.

"Dad, don't be weird, yes we have enough money... just be here around six, okay? If we're going to be late we'll call your cell—God!"

Ron Carson turns to see the water tower behind him and keeps checking it as a navigation point on their journey in towards the center of the lot, left—then right—then straight. The tower, a simple apparatus for creating water pressure is the highest structure on this flat parcel of land, and the visual focal point for all who come to visit, dream, work, plot, and scheme. It has stared down and looked over all for many decades.

Somehow, the tower is strangely comforting to this simple practical man, and when it falls out of sight he feels uneasy, a little too hemmed in by the large imposing soundstages. Adding to his edginess, the lot is far too quiet for such a historic and significant place, and he begins to think the hype and popularity of the great movie studio is all a charade. He wonders if they're here on the right day, or maybe worse yet, he wonders if his girls have been duped.

However, as they walk along, more and more people begin to appear and fill out the small avenues between the massive soundstages. The crowd tames the lonely echoes, making it feel more human and alive. Ron becomes more at ease as even larger groups of people arrive to populate the street.

"Busy crowds of people, this is what a movie studio should look like," Ron mutters to himself.

Little by little, though silently and smoothly, dozens upon dozens more find their way out of doorways into their path, crisscrossing in front of them. Now, instead of uneasy solitude, the family is slowed down by the steadily increasing crowds, and with every step it becomes more and more difficult to avoid bumping into them.

Nearing a turn in the street, a new wave of intense youth comes rolling around the bend, with many more going back in the opposite direction. In no time at all, the family trio feels like churning salmon, fighting up a fast, swelling, human river.

The crowds get more loud and aggressive, emerging from who knows where, shooting across their path, while countless others overtake them quickly from behind. It was as if a bell had rung at a hellishly overcrowded high school with its hurried students scrambling for a much needed summer vacation.

Ron tries to ask passers-by if this is part of a movie shoot or a fire drill, but none of the crowd pay him any mind. His words are drowned out as if he were in an echoing gymnasium filled with a thousand people.

He picks out a word or two here and there; "points— lunch—intellectual—property," but mostly it's an unintelligible wall of grating human noise.

Strangely, none of the churning, intermeshing throng bumps into one other, and just like bees in a hive the crowd behaves and moves as one. It's as if they'd rehearsed this highly orchestrated, chaotic dance for quite some time, for they seem to have perfected it with menacing-like precision.

The girls desperately try to act cool, hoping this is just one of those lame flash mob things they've seen on YouTube. Janice, his beautiful daughter, gets spun around by the commotion and drops her aloofness, revealing a near-panicked concern over the sudden and ever swelling crowds. A loud sound, real or imagined dizzies her, and after regaining focus, she notices that her cousin Courtney's shirt is slightly ripped, with blood running down her sleeve.

Janice turns and looks back, struggling to see her trailing father. Ron Carson raises his head up and catches sight of his pride and joy, then nods in fatherly reassurance as if to say:

"Not to worry my baby, I'm just steps behind and will soon hold your little hand in comfort."

Janice looks to him as she did when she was five

years old, riding her bike for the first time without training wheels, scared but ready for change, stepping towards maturity.

With the buzzing sweep of commotion all around him, a distance is forced between he and his babies and he loses sight of them. He catches just one last glimpse of Janice and Courtney, seemingly being hurried along by a group of smartly dressed people, turning left between four giant soundstages.

He attempts to follow but is almost run over by a fast moving camera truck blaring its horn, noticing at the same time that the massive crowds deftly and effortlessly jump back as the truck careens past them. Then, standing at the crossroads, turning, furiously twisting and looking for his girls, the crowds suddenly and strangely disperse, vaporize, snake away into doors, around corners, up stairs—leaving him standing alone with an awful, empty, sick feeling in his heart and stomach.

It was as if they were whisked away by a fast moving then suddenly vanishing human squall. He gently calls to them, but feels embarrassment, as surely no one in this place of importance ever shows any sign of weakness, sadness or worry.

CHAPTER 2

COME TO CALIFORNIA

A STRONG CRACK OF rare thunder shakes me wide-awake. It's raining again. Strangely, I see my recent life as a blue tinged outline, with capital letters and lowercase words indicating the path to the exact spot where I lay at the moment, taking stock of my situation—trying to figure out who I am.

What I know is this: I'm Truman Morrow, a forty-four-year-old male. I'm unmarried; I'm now unemployed, and I used to think I was very talented. I love good music, great movies, F. Scott Fitzgerald, subtle cologne, good leather boots, and fine living. I hate phonies (except real ones), bullies, thieves and hypocrites. I have been in Los Angeles for fourteen years and yesterday down by the river, I tried to kill myself.

Roberto, the very large man that pulled me in from the brink never questioned why I was going to do it—he never even asked me what had led up to it. He plainly told me that I was saved for a reason, and he had come to make me a deal, a *"grande* deal," as he put it.

I don't know if I passed out— I must have, because the next thing I knew, I was in my car, watching some gorgeous, uninvited, puffy clouds, push their way into our unemotional wide-open sky.

I'm a writer that left New York City for Southern California after having burnt out on New York, and its dark East Coast routine—its subways, its smells, its all too closed-in living arrangement. In Los Angeles, I was bent on reversing my shut-in, boring, dull brown, book-nook solitude.

My California adventure began when I was still living in New York. It was nineteen ninety-five, and I was just twenty-five years old. I got a job doing rewrites on my first feature film, a film that was shooting in Manhattan. This particular film was a smaller produc-tion, so it afforded me the opportunity to meet a lot of the cast and crew.

On the film's set, I met this talent manager from Los Angeles, an older woman of about seventy, named Mae McLaughlin. Mae was representing Ms. Erica Slayton, a gorgeous young actress with a small role in the film—an actress that I became intensely attracted to. Thankfully, both ladies took a liking to me, and we were able to spend a good amount of time together during their time in New York City.

"Erica, where do you live in California?" I asked as most New Yorkers do, ignorantly interchanging the city of Los Angeles and the state of California when referencing locations.

"I live in Beachwood Canyon," she said quite politely.

I nodded as if I knew where the hell Beachwood Canyon was. (Having never been to the West, whenever I heard the word canyon, I had always pictured Roy Rogers and coyotes.)

Erica had an understated infectious smile that cloaked an attractive seriousness—she was a fairly tall and healthy looking with chestnut hair, and had a sexy, calm way about her. She was fair-skinned with light freckled cheeks dancing high above her incredibly sexy body. And those eyes... Erica had the most piercing blue eyes, and I found myself unable to stop looking at them.

Like most really beautiful women, Erica seemed to be used to attention, but at the same time, there was a part of her personality that came off as a bit fragile and lost.

"So young man, you're a writer... are you any good?" her manager Mae abruptly asked.

When an older person says a challenging thing like this, I always cut them some slack, but in this case, I kept my wits about me and offered her a crafty answer.

"Well, Mae, if I weren't, we certainly wouldn't be working together on the same film, would we?"

As I answered her, I was once again staring at the

lovely Erica Slayton, who just softly smiled like a person that held many secrets.

"Very good, Truman... a pithy, enterprising answer. You may do well, son."

Mae raised her eyebrow and took a sip of her coffee. She then grabbed Erica by the arm, and pulled her towards a much more important meeting with the executive producer of the film.

In those two weeks, we dined as a trio, for Mae was hands-on and insisted on chaperoning her gorgeous young protégé nearly everywhere she went. It was a little strange and sometimes uncomfortable, but all in all we all had a wonderful time together. When they finally returned home, I made it a point to keep in touch with both ladies, Mae for business and Erica out of pure desire.

The night before they left, Erica and I slipped away without Mae, and had a quiet dinner alone in Chinatown. We ate at one of those authentic Chinese restaurants that always seem to be patronized by locals. After the slightly rude waiter had taken our order, Erica surprised me.

"Truman, do you like me?"

She seemed so innocent, even nervous when she wasn't being propped-up by Mae. I noticed that she had the habit of putting her hand to her mouth as if to cover up emotion or embarrassment. It was an endearing, old-time feminine motion. In my reply to her, I thought about playing it cool and coy, but I've never been a good liar.

"Are you kidding, Erica? My God—yes."

I sensed the moment had come to grab a first kiss from her, and after locking eyes; I leaned across the table and kissed her incredibly soft lips. Our mouths had a perfect meeting. No awkward head tilting, no tension, just a perfect poem of physical ease and human passion.

"Truman, will you come and see me out in LA?"

This time my answer was merely a very large honest smile.

The dinner was delicious, and afterwards we walked for hours, north from Chinatown, to Soho, and then up through Greenwich Village, finding a seat on a Washington Square Park bench to take in the sometimes bizarre, comings and goings of the West Village crowd in summertime.

On the way back towards her hotel, we walked by a trinket shop. In the window was a tray of costume jewelry, and in the center of that tray was a necklace with a small enameled Christmas tree hanging on it.

"Oh look at that, Truman, isn't that beautiful? There isn't a Christmas tree in the whole world that I don't love."

With that I pulled her into the still open shop and asked the owner if she could try it on. She put it around her neck and smiled big enough to light up the whole store. It goes without saying that the shop owner smiled as well, knowing full well that he could have his price.

She wore the little Christmas tree the rest of that night, a night that was unfortunately tainted by the unpleasant thought that she was going back to Los Angeles in the morning.

When her plane left and headed west, it might as well have flown through my heart, because after she'd gone, the days and weeks seemed so very hollow to me. Erica touched me and dusted my life with love, hope and happiness. I was bitten for sure. A few months later, after calling her daily and dreaming of her most every night, I decided I couldn't stand it any longer and needed to go out West for a visit.

When I got off the plane at Burbank Airport, I was taken by a vision of heaven—for there she was, framed by the sensuous Southern California night air, standing with a single rose at the outdoor baggage claim area. Her hair, skin and eyes were focused and lifted by the contrapuntal clanking machinery of the baggage carousel, and her very feminine gesture of putting her hand to her mouth told me that she was indeed glad to see me.

This surely was Erica's element, although beautiful in New York, here in California; she was absolutely radiant. My breathing stopped for a few seconds as I drank her in and said nothing for what seemed like an eternity—I was oblivious to everything and everyone around us. Then, with a teasing smile, she spoke volumes about what was to come that week.

I moved in close and put my arm around her waist,

letting it slide slightly lower to her hips. A soft kiss was all that we shared, but as a man, as a human, I couldn't have been more satisfied than I was in those few seconds, for all the joys of being alive awaited in those sweet eyes, all the promise of youth beckoned me to her sensuous skin and hair, and quite simply, in all my years, I'd never experienced such a romantic welcome.

Most fond memories are more than images; this vivid one rings alive in its smells, sounds and small details. Though I'm growing older, the moment is deeply engrained in my mind, and like an ageless elixir, it's one that I take in frequently, hoping that it will keep invigorating the young man that I once was.

"Let's go, Tru," she said, as she flipped her hair.

Then, grabbing my hand, she pulled me down into her California. She could have been taking me to hell, but it didn't matter—that girl was my life's thrill, and I was going to follow her anywhere.

My time spent with Erica on that trip was one of laughter and wild passion, our days in the sun, and nights in the perfumed cool air made it hard to return to the East the following week.

The incense she burned in her apartment, the rhythms of soulful music, and the lost hours of wonderful new restaurants with wonderful new people constructed a perpetual wizard's machine in my brain that tapped at my desire for her and her golden California.

Back in New York, I held both her love and the sun's warmth deep inside me for quite some time, and knew that I'd return soon to be with her and the West once more. My time spent with her manager, Mae McLaughlin, only increased that desire to return, for Mae spiked the intoxicating Southern California punch, adding glamorous parties, private screenings and much needed business connections to the mix.

Erica and I talked daily and wrote good old-fashioned love letters back and forth across the continent for several weeks. To soothe my longing for her, I sent her gifts, post cards and silly trinkets nearly every day. It was my way of staying in close touch, and it pacified my desire for the most exciting and beautiful woman that I'd ever met.

I'm sure you can imagine my disappointment when the late night phone calls and poetic letters from Erica abruptly stopped. Nothing showed up in the mail—the phone stopped ringing.

Adding to my sad confusion, her number had become disconnected, and though I tried many ways to find her, I knew it was over when several of the last little gift packages that I'd sent came back to my door unopened, scuffed-up, and stamped with the cold, iconic phrase—*Return To Sender*.

When I phoned Mae, her manager, she barked at me in a huff, saying that Erica "just up and left the business," hinting that she'd met some guy and "got into trouble, if you know what I mean."

I mourned her deeply and although I was no stranger to disappointment or loss of a relationship, no woman had ever affected me as Erica did. To add to my sorrow, jealousy was ignited by Mae's words. I wanted to find out who the man was. I wanted to ask her why she had broken my heart.

Erica was carefree, bright and had immediately carved out a unique place in my heart—a space that was shaped exactly in her image, and like any singular mold, she securely prevented anyone else from filling that space.

Erica was my attraction to the West Coast—she was the sunshine—she was the myth. Even after suffering her disappearance, I still decided to pack up my New York life and move to Los Angeles. Though some may have thought I was chasing her, she had sold me enough on Southern California to leave the East Coast and head west—whether she was there or not.

*

Another large, rare crack of thunder bends the bedroom window as only low frequency can. I gaze out of focus, fuzzy-green, lilting, and then shaking it off, straight ahead.

Growing tired of the popcorn-ceiling stare-down; I get up to make a cup of tea. Sometimes tea is just the thing, as it seems to fit perfectly between quiet moments and taste buds. I stir in the milk and continue my memories at the kitchen table. I feel like I've been asked to take a good look at my life, and if so, I'm quite comforted to see that it's still quite dark out.

CHAPTER 3

THE TOWN OF INSECURITIES

BACK THEN, WHEN I first arrived from New York, I behaved like a character actor playing a newly christened Baptist from an old silent movie. I was careful to stay away from all the places that Erica Slayton and I went to, but after leading what had become a grinding life in Manhattan, I was ready for fun.

When I first got here, Los Angeles certainly was fun—it was like high school with money, so I enrolled in my second adolescence, alone but happy, nestled into the soft slope of the Los Angeles basin. At first, I got a place in the fashionably trashy district called Fairfax, and cruised the streets and boulevards in an all-original 1964 Dodge. This car quickly became the chariot of my life's rejuvenation, and the bitchin' vessel of my recaptured immaturity.

Being a lover of vintage automobiles, it was a perfect fit for me, and it even had a period "Beach Boys" sticker in the back window. Its incredible interior was its finest feature, it was showroom perfect, and to ride in it was just about as close to time travel as you could get. The flashy new Ferraris on Sunset Boulevard had nothing on me, for they were a dime a dozen—I was the cheater of time.

At this point, living in Los Angeles felt so natural, almost as if I had lived here forever. Little by little, I found some new friends, and with them discovered a whole new social world.

There was Robert—he was so very good to me when I first came out to Los Angeles. He was my true pal, and did things for me because he wanted to. Robert never asked for anything in return. He had a heart of gold, and was one of the funniest people that I'd ever met.

Robert was a product of his Los Angeles environment and he knew it. He had a cell phone before they were commonplace, drove half a block to the supermarket and always spent more money than he had.

Eventually, Robert became an LA casualty and actually did something that most casualties don't do—he up and left. Usually casualties will get a few more tattoos, drink, drug, and hover somewhere under the radar. Robert had a purpose—he knew he had to get out of Los Angeles—he knew he had to save himself. Before he left, he gave me half of his possessions for my first apartment, and then ran off to London, never to return.

Another one of my new friends was Cassie. On the surface, she was a very affected young lady. Everyone that met her initially sized her up as just another run-in-the-mill phony actress, but that's who she *really* was—a true honest to goodness phony.

Yes, Cassie was full of crap most of the time, but it was completely real, and it came quite natural to her. Her over the top mannerisms and propped-up elitist conversation meshed perfectly with the sensuous night air surrounding every party we'd visit in those early, fun Hollywood nights.

One night after some hobnob, we were quite hungry and ended up in a dive of a Mexican restaurant on Sunset Boulevard. When we walked in, Cassie behaved as if we were entering the grand Hollywood affair of the century, with large dramatic hellos for the manager, waiters, even an effervescent "Hi!" into the kitchen. (I remember the blank stares from the sweaty wrung-out kitchen help.)

"Tru, isn't this place fab? Oh my goodness, you have to order *off* the menu. Don't even pick up the menu or they'll think we're tourists!"

Then she reduced her excitement to a stage whisper and added:

"Tru, do you have cash? I'm all out."

Cliff was a goofy sort, who just happened to be quite wealthy. He made his fortune in commodities back in the Midwest, then made up his Midwest mind to come out to Los Angeles and become a successful producer— just like that… no connections, no contacts, just a war chest, a gift for gab, and Midwest know-how. You know what? He did it.

Cliff showed his goofy side in the daytime by wearing calf-high socks and seventies-style shorty-shorts. In deeper evening conversations and more standard attire, he'd remind me that his five-year plan had him returning back to Chicago with several successful movies under his belt.

Like most producers, he was cocky and slightly obnoxious, but also quite love lost—yes, Cliff was a guy that had trouble getting on with women. Cliff wasn't homely or anything, I just think he was uneasy expressing the correct emotions that women are attracted to. He was a tad course and forward, with a personality geared more for business rather than romance. At times he seemed to cover up this shortcoming by holding a deep disdain for anyone with less business ambition than him.

"Don't you know where you're going... what's your five year plan?" he'd ask. When I'd change the subject to women, or anything else besides my plan for the future, he'd raise his chin up and tell me about a script or a prospect. Quite frankly, I always wanted him to read my scripts.

"Give me a few weeks," he'd tell me.

Let me translate, "give me a few weeks," means "hell never," anywhere outside of Los Angeles.

Cliff produced a couple of pictures, then with his growing success, and true to the way things go out here, I began to see less and less of him, and as you've probably guessed, he never responded to a single script I'd sent him.

Then of course there was Mae McLaughlin, Erica's manager—I never asked her about Erica again, I just couldn't bring myself to do so. Mae was framed differently in my life at that point and loomed quite large. She was my direct connection to connections, a ringleader of sorts because most of my social comings and goings spun right around her.

Mae would hold little parties—she would call them "greeters," and we'd all show up at either her place or a nearby valley restaurant, in desperate hope that she'd have someone there, someone that would help us leave our mortal lives and deliver us to stardom.

Without a doubt, my best companion was my friend and once upon a time fling, Sherry Cleveland. We came out West around the same time, and she too fell in with all my new hobnobbing pals. Sherry was absolutely gorgeous, her slender body, platinum blond hair and crystal blue eyes could halt a thrice-jaded man in his tracks. Her smoldering sexuality was always very carefully packaged in a neat, plain outfit, her perfect smile hovering just eight inches or so over very ample breasts.

We met in the fall of 1994 in New York when she was a model, made friends, and had a bit of an affair. I was riding in a down elevator when it stopped at the floor where her modeling agency was. In walked this vision of a woman.

"Hi, I'm Tru."

She looked me up and down, then coolly re-pressed the already selected ground-floor button. I felt like a fool for putting myself in harms way, but after ten floors of uncomfortable silence she turned and said:

"Yes… but will you be true blue?"

She smiled a very sexy half-smile, paused for a second as the doors opened, and then moved on as if I didn't even exist.

"Want to get a drink?" I asked, trailing after her like a little dog. "Or how about a coffee?"

She wheeled around, and after about five seconds of silent judgment, her stern look softened.

"Drink please," she said politely.

She took two steps back towards me, put her arm through mine, and finally let me take the lead. We walked off into a crisp Manhattan evening, and well, it was just one of those nights. I knew I had found an awesome companion.

Not long after that is when I'd met Erica, and after becoming head over heels crazy about her, Sherry sort of took a back seat. I guess Sherry did follow me out to Los Angeles, and probably wanted more, but I'd firmly planted the stamp of friend-with-benefits on her in order to concentrate on my precious writing career.

Sherry looked as if she belonged to another time, not retro in fashion, but in attitude—she was all-woman, without the slightest hint of self-consciousness or residual feminist shame for her unabashed classic femininity. This doesn't mean she wasn't without substance for

Sherry was extremely smart, holding a master's degree in English literature.

I've read some of her prose and poetry, and it's a shame that none of it's ever been published. I once asked her if she still had the desire to write, and she told me, "Only in my diary."

A year after college, the modeling agency swooped her up and got her a ton of work, and she quickly became the toast of the fickle model world for about six months or so.

Sherry had a charming way about her—a girl-next-door elegance that started a guy's brain ticking towards pipe and slipper land. She had a habit of touching the small silver cross that hung down low on her chest, almost as if she were pointing inward towards her heart, asking for you to come inside.

I'll be frank; Sherry's problem was that she came out to be a star actress, but brought only mediocre talent with her. With her less than lukewarm acting abilities, and propped up by stunning good looks, Sherry was ripe to fall victim to the vast system of treachery that was a natural byproduct of the entertainment industry.

As time went on, Sherry got involved with the wrong people—dark people, and was dabbling in a life-style of late-night clubbing, wild parties and all the illness that can creep into those dark corners.

When she began her slide, I would rescue her from time to time, hang out with her, comfort her, but after a while it became more and more difficult to be around her.

I could tell you more about Sherry, about our love-making, but that would be crude, about our day trips up to Santa Barbara, about our warm moments on my couch, just watching old movies, ordering in bad pizza, and falling asleep in each other's arms—but I won't. I can't even whisper anything but the utmost trivial details about her, for anything else would break my heart.

I've put my true feelings for Sherry away, high on a shelf, and though it's nice to know that they're there, most likely I'll never take them down again. Today, I merely dismiss her as an old acquaintance—a lost party girl.

What happened to Sherry really hardened me, because after Erica, she could have been the one. Sherry now lives just a few blocks away, and we do see each other occasionally. From time to time, I'll come to her aid, because even if I can't feel love for her, I can't help acting like her man. It's a tough spot to be in with a woman, and I pray for her all the time.

*

My tea's gone cold, but my kitchen's turned a warm yellow in the sun's first light. Like the morning after a car accident, the jolting memory of the giant man at the river is disturbing.

Punctuating the unpleasantness is the pain in my

ribs, placed there by his forceful grip. I sit still, trying to find answers, and continue my assessment of my West Coast life.

*

Perception is everything, and in those early days, my Los Angeles social barometer ignored all of the pitfalls of the fair weather and the high times. My social status was a role, and I was deep in it, playing it well and having a great time. So, with my youthful spark rekindled, I carefully pulled out, cleaned off and pressed my old suit of popularity that I had put away when I rounded the age of twenty-one.

Dropping some weight, and with a perky new swing in my step, it wasn't long before my new friends and I were moving in a well-heeled extended circle. In no time, we began taking in private first-run screenings, dinners on the arm, decent plays, half of boring plays, five and a half innings of Dodger games, and lush, slow, umbrella-shielded weekends at someone's mansion in Palm Springs. There was always some party to go to, some screening to attend, an invite to either the Playboy mansion, or a private room at a top-notch restaurant.

My Los Angeles honeymoon was way on. I was having so much fun that it was hard to believe that just a few months before, I was two-book-a-month, Upper East-Sider, shut up in a dark New York apartment. I used to brandish and shoot the "It's rent stabilized" fire extinguisher on any four-thousand a month Greenwich

Village jerk that told me the Upper East Side was boring. Now looking back on it, it wasn't the Upper East Side that was boring—I was the one who was boring.

Reversing my literary habits, I didn't read many books in the first few years out here and realized that I was in jeopardy of joining the ranks of the shallow, but for the time being I was just fine with it. With all my books stored away in boxes, I went out with Cassie, Cliff and Robert and of course Mae, from invite to invite, party to party, weekend to weekend, fete to fete.

With all this recreation, I found out pretty quickly that Hollywood clicks have some strict rules. So much of what goes on in Hollywood happens in a social situation, so being that I wanted my attraction and prowess to blossom, I needed to grasp the rules of these parlor games rather quickly.

One of the first rules I learned is to never say no in Hollywood. "No," is too final, and nothing in this town is ever really totally final. Final is forever, and forever is too much of a commitment for nervous opportunists fearful for their very own survival. In Hollywood and its vicinities, when and if the power shifts and the low man rises to the top, you don't want to be the fool that told him no.

At one of those early hobnobs, I struck up a conversation with a very famous but down-to-earth, director about his take on the rules of social maneuverings. He too was a former New Yorker, and was kind enough to lay it out in a parlance that cut right to it.

"Truman, it's good that you're out here. Let me chip away all the California bullshit for you. Out here you'll have so much smoke blown up your ass, that you'll probably get ass cancer. Most of these bastards will have you believe that they're geniuses, but making a movie is kind of like working on a science project with all of the big words removed.

"Truman, when find yourself on a big picture, and you eventually will—you'll quickly note that there's no tyranny quite like the movie business. They'll tell you there's this rule, and that rule, but let me set you straight——these are the only real rules you need to know:

One. No one invited you.

Two. No one cares that you're here.

Three. No one will care if you leave.

Buddy, if you can deal with those three rules, then you'll be just fine here."

At first I was a little taken aback by these words. I felt like I'd just been slapped and pushed at the same time, but after a while, I understood that he was merely telling me that this town was a dog-eat-dog, every-man-for-himself, make-it-what-you-will, kind of town—and he was absolutely dead-on.

Complicating it all is the sad fact that no one really wants you to become successful, even most of your friends, unless of course, they can own a piece of you, and if that's the case, you and your success will become very popular indeed.

This is a town of insecurities. For the most part, people want what they can't have, and don't want what they can have. Insecurity is a major motivational force here, and it's no wonder because the molecular design of desire includes a healthy portion of masochism. Seeking, searching, dreaming, crying, are very familiar behaviors for showbiz folks. Wanting is unfulfilled having, and no one in this town ever thinks they have enough.

So now, with these rules packed way down into my suddenly re-proportioned Hollywood brain, I had a choice; get back on the plane and go read musty old books, or plunge waist deep into the social scene and try to make something happen.

Swaying my decision was an invitation through Mae to attend some weekly first-run screenings at the very fashionable Bel Air home of Lawrence Fischer, head of the biggest movie studio in town. Fischer was a powerful man, the club that wouldn't let you in, and he left us all wanting more. Wine, caviar, glamorous women, famous stars... it was all happening at the home of Lawrence Fischer. I eventually ended up working at his movie studio, but at his parties, I never got to say more than a quick hello.

One night it seemed he was quite upset with Mae McLaughlin and there was a heated exchange. After exiting his home, a very tipsy Mae, turned to me and said:

"You know, Tru, nothing is free in this town... nothing at all."

I thought it was very curious, mainly because it was the first and only time I'd ever seen Mae with her tail between her legs.

I was living the life, and the invites were coming fast, but at this point my wallet couldn't support even a subsidized invitational lifestyle. So just about six months into being on a first-name basis with the best chefs in town and receiving far too many valet parking dents, I knew that I needed to be just a little more practical and find a new, less expensive place to live.

I would have liked to remain fashionable and keep a 310 or a 213 area code, but when you're living off of savings, you take the valley, and its 818. The response to my decision to move to the valley prompted several of my most insanely hip friends to protest:

"Dude, why are you moving to the valley?"

Alas, when you move over the hill, you'll become unfashionable to some and will be downright excommunicated by others. The latter didn't matter to this well-grounded boy, for I chose a lovely two-bedroom townhouse apartment in a very affordable part of North Hollywood.

Mae was the one who told me about the place, in fact, it was right there in her building. A vacancy had come up—I called the moving van, and off we went, over the hill. The place was nice, the price was right, and I think Mae enjoyed having me close by.

Dear sweet Mae—she was a San Fernando Valley girl from way back, and I miss her. When she died two years ago, her funeral had a line of visitors stretching out the door—a line sprinkled with some pretty famous and important faces... even Lawrence Fischer's.

*

Lightning flashes again, this time with no report. I look out the kitchen window and wonder at the silent movement of the rarely seen storm clouds.

This morning my block is quiet, my building quieter, and with no one coming or going it leaves me to wonder if anyone in my complex ever goes to work. It's always amazed me how many people in this haltingly bright town have absolutely no visible form of employment.

Speaking of employment, I always thought that I was pretty good writer, but year after year, blow after blow, the spark of the young wordsmith was beaten out of me. When you're watching television and one of the shows you've written comes on, it should be a thrill. However, when your name is nowhere in the credits, you tend to remember that moment with less than a smile.

Several things like this happened to me, and before I knew it, I was off the A-list, behind on my rent, and hanging out in less than fabulous places. The resilient buffer that youth placed around my heart had eroded away. And so, I tumbled down, knee-deep into the LA malaise, without really knowing how I'd gotten there.

Initially I came out West with a burning business ambition, and then slowly, year after year, the flame was doused down to a smolder by my Hollywood *not-so*-merry-go-round. I almost didn't even notice that most of my friends had gone.

Cassie had moved on with the mega-bucks man of her life and was now a semi-permanent resident of Palm Springs. Cliff finished his five-year plan, quit producing and did indeed move back to Chicago. Robert, is still somewhere in London, and of course, dear Mae, has passed on.

I don't want to think about all this, but after my episode down at the river, I guess this introspective inventory of my life is a natural thing. I remember Charlie…

"This town, it's a circle," this drunk at a bar told me. "One day you're in the circle, and you spin around, richer than shit, then one day—you're out on your ass."

I remember thinking at the time that this rosacea-faced inebriated man was probably just a bitter old grip or camera assistant. A few weeks later, back at the same bar, I overheard the bartender talking to another patron about him.

"Did you hear about Charlie? Yeah he killed himself last week—I can't believe it—found him with his head in the oven. Charlie was a big television director back in the sixties and seventies."

I guess Charlie had enough of being down and out,

or maybe he just had no family or friends. I found out his last name and looked him up online. Charlie was something in his day, with twenty-five years of steady work listed in his credits. We all raised a toast to Charlie, and for a long minute after—the bar was entirely silent.

My reason for attempting suicide wasn't just the fact that I had become persona non grata amongst the hip and happening. It wasn't the lack of work, or my thinning friends. It wasn't the Christmas Eve's alone, or the dinners-for-one, for all that can be tolerated when you expect that a better day will soon come your way. If I had to point to a main reason for my desperation, it would be simply be, as I have previously mentioned—a complete absence of hope.

*

The rain gets louder against the side of the townhouse, accompanied by another loud thunderclap. I'm stuck, gun-shy, and scared, wondering what month my bank account will run out. I'm coasting on it, and it's just a matter of time.

I have an old Life magazine from the 1940s. Inside there's a photo spread on living in the San Fernando Valley; California's booming new suburb. The photos are bitterly comforting, ex-servicemen coming out West after the war, and flying by the seat of their pants into the post-war boom of Southern California.

Gas stations, beautiful ones with large glass-topped "visible" pumps out in front, handled by men who wore gray hats against deep blue skies, ones that smiled at your kids and filled your tires. Gas 'er up and drive through orange groves, peach groves, new farms, new construction, boom, people—come live the good life in the golden San Fernando Valley.

They say this valley was once a sea. Fossils of fish have been found in the canyons where drivers carelessly skid off the road when it rains. The valley was once home to content people who ate what they killed and harvested, and lived solely for the beauty of life and family.

Today it's filled with people who want all they can get from life right now, and will do what it takes to get it faster and easier than the other guy. They swim through the narrowing canyons of materialism and race each other to the exit, for here in material land, he with the most stuff wins. Everyone here is so afraid to be who they are, so they pose to prosper. I for one would love to be myself... if I could just figure out who I am.

Thunder shakes the room. This storm is raging again. As it often does, my mind drifts back to the memories of the one who brought me here, Erica—the one whom I'll forever secretly look for in shopping malls, libraries, and grocery stores.

I rise and head for the shower as the lights flicker and the power goes out. Electric hot water—I'd better hurry.

*

Dear Diary, May 28

You just called to see how I'm doing in the storm. I pretend not to be thrilled, but it's an act. You're my Scarecrow, Truman Morrow. I can only tell you this here, in my lonely old diary, the one with far too many tear marks bumping up the yellowed thin paper. On this ridiculous journey through our troubles, you protect me with your silent strength; you sing to me with your lost voice, you comfort me with your guiding thoughts.

The fact that you can't be with me is the most bittersweet poetry of all, and it causes me, even in sadness, to love you all the more.

– Sherry Cleveland

CHAPTER 4

ROLLING WITH THE TUMBLEWEEDS

THERE'S SUCH A thing as being honest to a fault, and not putting up a good front most assuredly is at the root of many a Hollywood failure. When I truthfully tell people that I need work, it is perceived as a weakness, a weakness that is not fashionable, desirable or attractive. Honesty used to be considered a virtue, and maybe it still is in some places, but certainly not in this town when it comes to business.

Since this industry's product is based predominantly on fantasy, conjecture and imagination, it is not much of a surprise to find out that all those attributes have become ingrained into every aspect of the business, in front of and behind the camera. There are multi-million dollar deals that hang in the balance, poised perfectly and based solely on complete fabrications. Lying, half-truths and trickery are essential elements in our business, and those that master them will usually reap the rewards.

To wit:

- There's a producer that's desperately trying to cast his picture with two big movie stars, both who've already turned him down. He instructs his long-suffering assistant to call each of the stars separately, and tell them both that the other star has already agreed to be in the picture. Lying brings on insecurity.

- There's a screenwriter that tells everyone at every party that she did all of the unaccredited writing for a certain blockbuster, when she never wrote a single word. Lying brings about notoriety.

- There's a well-known costume designer that doesn't design anything he works on, one who'll employ some underlings to design and make the costumes for the producer's movie. Lying provides jobs.

- The producer knows the designer is lying about making the costumes, but is still okay with it as long as the well-known designer's name is listed in the credits. He then hires that lying screenwriter that he met at the party because she's sleeping with and was recommended by the one movie star, who is now considering co-starring in the picture because he bought the lie about the other movie star agreeing to co-star in the picture.

- The producer then curtly demands that his

long-suffering assistant pull all the strings to all these lies at the same time. If the pull is quick, and all the lies line up correctly; then what falls down in the producer's lap is sure to be a hit.

- In a stunning development, just prior to the film's release, the long-suffering assistant is suddenly promoted to the position of co-producer, for it seems that during the entire production, he was well aware that his abusive boss was having a torrid sexual threesome with both of the movie stars' wives.

Lying is a fundamental part of the entertainment culture, and it occurs at all levels. If you want to be successful here, you better practice it and perfect it. Hollywood is what you make it, and unless you make out that you are making it, you will never make it at all.

Once again the rain has stopped, so after my third cup of tea and some underdone wheat toast, I attempt to rejuvenate my positive can-do attitude (aka lying like hell), with a vigorous walk around my neighborhood.

Now just so you know, only licensed-deprived traffic scofflaws, criminals, junkies and weirdoes walk around in the valley. Fitting snuggly into group four, I take my weirdo exercise daily, walking the wide, weed-strewn sidewalks of Lankershim Boulevard northward from my condo, all the way up across Magnolia Boulevard.

This town I live in was previously called "Lankershim," long before it was ever made-over with the more recent moniker of "North Hollywood." The latter, current name was the let's-cash-in-on-Hollywood idea arrived at by some of its woefully misled elders back in the 1930s.

I continue on past the Television Academy, where Lankershim had its town square. In this square was a small but beautiful rose garden, where the old roses, hybrids, and teas stood straight, proud and silent. The conditions for growing roses were as perfect then as they are now, with full sun and long hot days, almost as if God made California just for the roses, and let humans in merely to take care of them.

Just past the garden, were the tracks for the tidy and punctual Red Car. The Red Car was the wonderful local rail line that was killed off by the automobile lobby and Southern California progress. Some say the loss of the Red Car was a terrible blow for this valley, the quintessential sad marker of its decline, and the turning point to becoming the orange-smog, car-crunched, freeway capital of the world. Few realized at that moment that a great neighborhood was rolling over and falling slowly, like a lifeless fish, thrown back too late into a dark summer lake.

As I walk along the weed-strewn sidewalks on the west side of the boulevard, I come upon Trader John's Record Store. I used to be a steady customer, but hadn't stopped in for a few years. I was surprised and happy to see that he was still in business. John's is a little old storefront putting up a valiant effort, carrying on in spite of the small customer base for pressed vinyl.

Parked out front is a gorgeous classic car, the unmistakable 1939 Lincoln Zephyr Coupe. Although it's not in *le cercle de concours d'elegance* number one condition, it's certainly someone's prized possession all the same, with original interior and what looks to be all-original paint. It must be owned by one of John's customers because if I remember correctly, John drives a ratty old wreck.

One of my prized possessions I brought with me from New York is my 1956 Seeburg 100-J Jukebox. It would be nice to have some new forty-fives for my old mechanical wonder, so I decide to stop in for a visit, inquiring of a very lovely thirty-something redhead if John is in.

"Sorry, John is no longer here, I own the store now, can I help you sir?"

Calling me *sir*, tells me that she's grown tired of having to dispense with the former owner and assert her rightful ownership. It also might have helped if I tidied up a little more this morning, but being light on my feet when the occasion is conversing with a lovely woman, I snap-to and focus like a laser on crafting a retort so witty and disarming that she will instantly ignore my slightly shabby morning appearance in order to see the shining, fun, handsome guy that I truly am.

"Oh, okay... cool," I say.

Obviously bowled over by this nimble display of Noel Coward charm, she adds:

"I'm Jane Axton... don't mean to be too formal. Is there anything you're interested in mister...?"

"Oh, I'm Truman Morrow, but please, call me Tru. Yes, in fact, you can help me. I'm looking for the forty-five of Nat King Cole's "Stardust"—it may be scarce."

She walks over to the "C" labeled record bin and betrays her lack of confidence in the possibility of fulfilling my request by forming a clenched smile, then raising her hand to her mouth, and shaking her gorgeous red hair in a soft "no" motion.

We are not alone; there are nosey bodies about—Dylan, The Beatles, and Elton records peek over the tops of their bins, inquisitively staring out from the surrounding aisles.

"I don't think I carry that, but I can do a search and then order it for you."

She looks at me, and we share a smile. It was just a short look, but not an ordinary one—it was one of those looks, the kind that begin relationships. Yes, she's gorgeous, sweet, and she looked at me.

What she's done to Trader John's is miraculous. It's so neat and clean, like a Protestant musical church, with some of the best and most rare albums I've ever seen in one collection. The store is strange and hauntingly beautiful in its simplicity with scented candles and dim lights highlighting her obvious deep reverence for the recordings. You'll never find this when you download digital music.

"Yes sure, please order it for me."

I turn around to see Coltrane and Chet Baker album covers coolly sneering at me from the "Blue Note" section. I can't tell if they approve of my order.

"Okay, I'll find it for you. My search fee is seven dollars and fifty cents, then there's the cost of the record. It could end up being about twelve to fifteen dollars."

"Oh that's fine, what's a few bucks for one of the greatest recordings ever made?"

"I know," she says. "The strings, that voice, and those romantic lyrics—kind of perfect, isn't it?"

A twinkle. There's a twinkle in her smile. Immediately I feel certain chemicals coursing through my veins. Natural chemicals, the ones created normally in a satisfied persons brain. I smile back, a real smile, not an LA smile at all. It's one of those warm involuntary ones. However, I do notice there is something peculiar about her face—at certain angles she looks like a mannequin.

"Okay, well… cool. I'll be coming in more often. It was really nice to meet you."

Man what a linguist. I should work for the United Nations. Knowing that too much of my witty charm might put her off, I back-pedal towards the door.

"Tru, wait, I'll need your number, and a deposit. Sorry, this is Los Angeles."

That's interesting—maybe her LA honeymoon has also come to an end.

"Oh, sure, let me give you some cash," I tell her.

"Five dollars will do," she politely adds.

And then I see it. With the help of the light that shines through her store windows, I notice that one of her eyes is quite different. It appears to be a perfect glass copy of its mate. My assessing glance is short, but when she drops her gaze to my mouth, it tells me that she's noticed my discovery. I feel bad. I want to tell that it doesn't matter... I want to say that imperfect is very sexy.

"Are you in the business?" she asks. "I sell a lot of records to the prop departments on all the lots. Just curious if you're an actor or something."

Most people are only interested in the sizzle of the business, the drama, the stars and the parties. Whenever one of us behind the scenes folks chats on about what we do, attention drifts and wild parties come to an end.

"Oh, I'm a writer," I tell her. Then, in nearly the same breath add, "Hey is that your '39 Zephyr out front?"

"Wow, Tru—you know your cars, it sure is."

A record store, a '39 Zephyr, and an approachable, imperfect, sexy woman—I think smitten is the appropriate word here.

I leave the store and look back in the window. She gives me a nervous kind of wave, then a coy smile—the kind of smile that shows a connection. Liking that, I'm lighter in my step, and the ordinary amble down the weedy sidewalks of the grey boulevard becomes quite enjoyable.

Coming towards me down the street is an old, blue pickup truck carrying mattresses. It's plodding along, and hanging low on its rear axle.

He does exist—it's him again... the man who saved me, I excitedly think to myself.

The old mattresses are piled high, just like in the children's story. The engine is exhausting some blue oily smoke, and the straw-hatted, olive-skinned driver smiles at me as he drives past... but this time it's not the giant Roberto. It's someone else.

I walk on to do some shopping, navigating the wrappers, bottle caps and aforementioned growth on the nobody-walks-in-the-valley sidewalks. The wind blows, informing the trees of what they are, then moves the resting grit from its comfortable corners out into the street, only to be scattered by the passing traffic. A large weed that was most likely dismembered from its roots somewhere out in the desert, blows along the sidewalk, rolling next to me as I walk along.

It's a tumbleweed—an actual tumbleweed, and I playfully think to myself that it's here to accompany me, a lonesome pioneer, as I bravely stroll out into the Wild West.

I travel on to round up some groceries at the local market (healthier, fat reducing items, so I can look good at the record store), and turn back up the boulevard to find my way home. Walking along, I see the same old mattress pickup truck parked across the street. The strange driver is arranging the mattresses on the back of the truck and talking into a shiny silver cell phone that looks as though it's highly polished chrome.

Why the heck would they be hauling around old mattresses? Do they sleep on them? Are they selling them? I see them on the freeways, I see them on the boulevards, and I see them in alleyways and parking lots.

As soon as I got home, in Jane Axton's honor, I polished up the jukebox and listened to some of my great old records. Later, I just watched some television. A good way to hasten and/or advance your rut is to entrench yourself in a non-productive routine, and it seems that in my fourteenth year here in Los Angeles, I have that down to a science.

I don't really remember going to my bed or falling asleep, I just remember opening a second beer, settling back down on the couch… and trying to count all those tumbleweeds.

*

Dear Diary, May 30

Truman told me about a dream he had. He dreamt of tumbleweeds clogging Lankershim Boulevard, parting for then rolling on behind this lady's old car. He waved to her, but the woman

that waved back was elderly and unrecognizable.
He said he then walked through the old town
of Lankershim, back before it had become the
decaying North Hollywood — back with the scent
of orange trees — back in the sunshine before some
ether-cameraman inserted a dirty, smudged,
orange lens.

He said a woman, young and beautiful,
walking like a ghost through the rose garden
in the center of town, was radiant in a glowing
twilight. She then turned to him and whispered
her long-held secret...

He said he awoke at that point, but I think he
just didn't want to tell me the rest.

— Sherry Cleveland

CHAPTER 5

JUNE GLOOM

I AWAKE TO MY head feeling jagged and angular, as if sharp light has bounced in and around it all evening. My eyes are reluctant to start the day, but like a rusty old trunk I pry them open.

There are six apples on my footboard. Six shiny pieces of fine produce just beyond my toes are what fill my gaze this morning. Although I did have a couple of beers last night, it certainly wasn't enough alcohol to inspire a minimalist's fruit arrangement at the foot of my bed. The apples are in perfect alignment as if some boring haircut came in overnight and carefully set them up just so, making sure all of their little stems pointed in the same direction.

Rising to get some breakfast, I notice that there are six eggs in the refrigerator. This isn't very unusual save for the plain fact that they look much neater than this bachelor would ever set them—all with their small ends up. I'm beginning to get the feeling that someone deliberately was trying to attract my attention. I turn on the news, the morning newscaster is going on and on about the possibility of six dollar gas. Already twice bitten, this too catches my pricked-up ear.

Then, there are six pieces of junk mail arranged so perfectly that it has me envisioning a blue ghostly hotel maid, most certainly lost, straightening a much lesser address than she's used to.

Six pieces of bread left.

Six paintings on my walls.

Six napkins in the holder.

Six candles on the coffee table.

I didn't hear the cell phone ring all night long, but there are six new messages ready to be listened to. I press play on my first voicemail and hear nothing but a strange machine-like drone. I punch at the button on the phone advancing on to each of the next five messages—all the same. Every message shares the identical curious and disturbing noise.

I look over and see that an envelope has been put under my door. It looks to be made out of very old paper, and it's affixed with a red wax seal. I open it up to find the note inside brittle and written in an old style hand.

You are required to be at the crossroads of Lankershim and Vineland Boulevard, at ten o'clock this morning. Some will be easy – some will be hard.

My cell sounds six quick rings. The last one seems to bear an exclamation point that triggers the nasty jagged light in my head to begin bouncing around once more.

"Well… sometimes the phone company has special ring patterns for sales calls," I wishfully think.

I take a deep breath to calm my angst, but my breathing isn't progressing past the nervous, shallow kind. I pick up the phone, hoping to hear about a special offer on cell service, but instead hear the same droning noise in the background.

"Who the hell is this?" I yell into the phone. Then stomping over to the window, I notice there's one of the old pickups with mattresses, parked right across the street. No one is in the truck.

"Is anyone there?" I inquire, secretly hoping there's no answer.

A tedious ten seconds of drone drags on as I listen intently for some clue in the noise.

"I am… Armando."

The simple reply frightens the crap out of me, for it sounded like something out of a Hitchcock movie, where ordinary people are always more frightening than made-up monsters. The voice is deep and assured, with a stern Latino accent.

"I give you the note from Roberto… he's busy. You must to be at the Lankershim and Vineland Boulevard crossroads, some will be easy—some will be hard."

My heart races as I look back out to the street, for

the same man that I saw earlier comes out from behind his truck. He's much smaller than Roberto, almost tiny, but dressed in a similar fashion. This Mattress Man exudes a patient type of calm as if he owns the ground he walks on. As if by radar, he wheels around and looks straight up at me.

My heart pumps even harder and pushes the jagged blue light out of my head. Now, finally being able to focus, I bolt out of my condo door and make my way towards the street. I look up and down the block but find no one. No pickup truck, no mattresses, no straw-hatted driver, only the cool, overcast first day of June.

I'm beginning to remember more about my morning at the river, and now recall being led back to my car by the giant Roberto. I remember he said those same words, "Some will be easy—some will be hard." I also remember Roberto asking me for help—something about helping the people of the valley. I remember now, the *"grande* deal" he offered me—it was a deal to save my life.

Usually I embrace the coming of June in Southern California, with its overcast skies and cool air bringing a welcome break from the burning sun, but in this four-teenth year of my residency I nervously wonder; what in hell has this June gloom brought me?

Dear Diary, June 1

I interrupted Tru's morning with one of my

7:30 a.m. "I forgot where I parked my car last night, please come and get me," rescue calls. He came and got me from some hellhole in Reseda and took me home. He didn't ask any questions about whom I was with, or what I had done. I'm glad he didn't, because I would've lied to him. I'd like to say that I was embarrassed when I saw him, but survival and just the pleasure of being with him, quickly supplanted any feelings of discomposure.

I remember the ride home – the cool mist from the June morning pouring in his old car's vent windows, cooling my legs as it circled around and around.

Once home, I tried my best to bring him into my bed for morning comfort, but he gallantly tucked me in and softly kissed my forehead, then leaving me to my hangover, he went on with his day.

We live in a city where chivalry and gallantry are unappreciated. I certainly hope that one day, Truman will benefit from his beautiful ways and that leaving me this morning will bring him good fortune.

– Sherry Cleveland

CHAPTER 6

VISIONS OF LANKERSHIM, CALIFORNIA

I'M EATING ONE of the six apples. It tastes normal. I don't know what I was expecting, but it really tastes just fine. After a few bites, I realize I'm not at all hungry, and note that it's nine thirty. I've decided that I am indeed going to cruise by the intersection mentioned in the letter's instructions. So, if I'm to keep that appointment, I'd better get a move on.

My first thought is that this could be a plot, a possible kidnapping plot. After taking just about two more seconds to rationally think that through, I come to my senses and say aloud:

"Who in hell would want to kidnap an out of work, forty-four year-old single guy?"

In addition, on the odd chance that something bad does happen to me, I'd still be in the San Fernando Valley, with its grand total of fourteen kind and caring people in the entire population. Most likely, the pleasant valley folk will calmly whiz by and flip me the finger if I dare impede any of them from their self-actu-alized lives.

I drive past the big studio and see the old iconic water tower, and it practically smiles at me like an old friend. I certainly miss all the fun I had on that lot at one point in my career, I worked on two television series and two movies there. One of the television series was a non-starter, dead before airing due to internal studio power politics.

We were all sworn contractually to super-secret silence concerning the failure of that show, mostly because there was a star's reputation at stake. However, there's no secrecy when it comes to failure in Hollywood, and once the potential profitability of a person has been compromised (i.e., they're all washed up), the failures of one become the bragging rights of ten others.

One-upsmanship is a readily used lever in this town, and this star was rarely ever heard from again, except of course for the drunk driving, pill-popping arrest and well publicized, pathetic mug shot.

It's funny, but I respected him more in his failure than I did in any show he'd ever starred in. He showed me a true human condition, and although he wasn't pic-tured in the best light, I finally saw him as a real person with real feelings and problems. I felt so bad for him, and to this day I do wish him well. Another Hollywood lesson learned: Success loves popularity… failure hates it.

I'm not sure if I believe in ghosts, but I know that something sinister has dogged me at certain times in my life. Occasionally, it has seemed that there's been an unseen force nibbling at my heels, making me turn left when I should have gone right, prompting "yes" when it should have been "no," enticing me to go to a hobnob in Palm Springs, when I should have bumped into the love of my life at the local grocery store.

I guess you could say that bad luck is somewhat like a ghost, and like any ghost worth its salt, it's one that you'll never, ever see. It can change the course of your life, and recently it's brought this former alter boy down to his knees. I've been praying and asking for guidance, but sadly of late, I hear nothing but my own heartbeat.

I pass the restaurant where Mae used to hold her greeters, the place is still going, but I rarely see any of that group anymore. The only one that I see on a semi-regular basis is Sherry Cleveland. Every so often, I'll go to her place and take care of her cats when she leaves town, but as I mentioned, I really don't want to start seeing too much of her again. Sherry has become like one of those old songs you used to love that now has grown tiresome. When you hear those on the radio—you quickly turn to something else.

I pass the fringes of Toluca Lake, a lovely little community between North Hollywood and Burbank. My old friend Tom lived there. Tom was a screenwriter, an old-school typewriter man who shunned any use of a computer. He wasn't one of my hobnobbing pals; he was kind of my San Fernando Valley surrogate father, who helped me with my transition away from the harmful lights of Sunset Boulevard.

His house was a meeting and greeting place for the C-listers and wanna-bees, and at that point, I fit right in. We shared laughs, drinks, food and the pretense that we were all still thriving in the movie business.

Tom had every script he had ever written, piled up along his walls, and to look through them was like an archeological dig, the deeper you went the older and more yellowed the scripts were. Tom never married or had any kids, he lived a simple life, and although there were plenty of women interested in his day, like many old show folk, he had given his life to Hollywood.

For a while, he had some nephews that he talked about, but I think they ran afoul of the law back in Chicago because I noticed that he had taken their pictures down and didn't speak of them much anymore. As he grew frailer, I tried to take him out as much as I could, to a diner or a coffee house—Tom didn't go in for anything too fancy. He was a simple man that lived in a box, content to live out his time and silently hold on to his life's stories.

Tom sat night after night, staring at the television, surrounded by walls of his work, scripts that could have been stored away in boxes, hidden in closets, but never were—they were with him on Christmas Eves, Halloweens and Thanksgivings, and were only moved from display when they came to take his body away.

I arrived too late to say goodbye to him. In fact by the time I'd heard, his place was already cleared out and freshly painted. No one called me, but then again we didn't share too many friends. His landlord told me that his nephews came along with his brother and his wife, and that gave me comfort. He was cremated, and they took the ashes with them back to the Midwest.

Tom knew who he was, and never pretended to be anyone else, long ago accepting that Hollywood would leave him behind someday, alone there with his yellowing pages.

Coming upon the intersection, everything looks perfectly normal. There are cars whizzing through one way, then at the change of the light, blasting off from the other. I catch the green light and drive through, passing the large intersection with no occurrence, no bright lights or spacemen, no strange colors or sounds. I keep the intersection in my rear view mirror, just in case someone is following me then swing around at the next intersection, and head back once again towards my target.

Up to this point I feel silly and wonder once again if this is some sort of strange elaborate prank, but as my aging '64 Dodge gets closer to the intersection, this time—strange things do begin to happen. All of the traffic traveling with me begins peeling off left and right, turning down this street and that. In the rear view mirror, cars start receding as if being swallowed up by the cool, overcast June morning.

I slow down the car when I notice an older woman standing on the corner of La Maida Street and Lankershim Boulevard, just one block north of my destination. She's the spitting image of the dearly departed Mae McLaughlin—which of course is impossible. Reality screams that this can't be her; however, this is fast becoming anything but reality, and as surreal as it sounds, I'm very sure that it really is her.

Time feels as if it's stalling on me, and for a second, I wonder if I am going to pass out. Mae's face grows large and distorted in the center of my vision and I try to blink her away, but can't.

I know I have to concentrate on the road, but I'm no longer holding the steering wheel—I'm floating towards Mae with absolutely no control over my body. Turning my head, I see my driverless Dodge moving on like a mechanical ghost in the June morning.

All normal valley sound has ceased—there's no traffic noise—no helicopters, no sirens—nothing. I move closer to her, suspended in what appears to be bright water... closer and closer, her face getting larger and larger like in a funhouse mirror. She smiles at me and raises her perfect old hand in a queen-like wave of honest affection, her image soft and warm looking like an old lost relative from a sixties super-eight color movie. It feels as if I've been slipped some strong psychotropic drug, but still, I'm relaxed in its soft tide—calm and happy.

I'm moving in and out of her beating eyes like a rock falling into a clear, still pond. She floats weightlessly in a bath of warm bright colors, mixed with swirling heat. I hear her heart beating—she's alive—right here. Her eyes pulse with her heartbeats, brightening each time, in gorgeous red, swirling light.

The light begins to paint a picture and I begin seeing our old parties by the pool with crazy neighbors and potted palm trees in large red plastic pots by the garage. I see Mae introducing me to several prominent people that really kick-started my career. I remember the garage clicker on my car key ring, and can hear the sound of that big closing garage gate.

I try to shake myself out of it, blinking my eyes again in an attempt to do so. With each blink I'm back in the Dodge, and looking in the rearview mirror see myself as a younger man, passionately kissing two women—first Erica Slayton, and then after another hard blink, Jane Axton from the record store.

I turn around to look at them in the back seat but suddenly find myself walking in the middle of the boulevard without a soul around in what is all at once a quiet, overcast city. The street beneath my feet narrows and turns into a smaller dirt road, with a banner, hanging overhead, *1922 Peach Festival—Lankershim California*.

There are no large buildings around now, just a few homes off in the distance. I look up and down the boulevard and see dust blowing several large tumbleweeds across the road, filing them like envelopes between houses and shacks that sparsely populate the stillness of the 1920s.

Mae is standing across the road in an empty lot amongst some weeds, younger and quite attractive, albeit with a darker look about her. She smiles and with a short exhalation of breath, jerks her head slightly, almost mocking my appreciation of her beauty.

Before she was a manager, Mae was a producer in the business for many years, and rumor has it that early on she was none other than Clark Gable's mistress. Mae McLaughlin knew so many people, from Jack Warner to Spielberg, Eastwood to Tarantino, Bob Hope, and even Elvis.

Power is essential in Hollywood, and Mae understood how it could and should be wrangled. Knowing these people was her base of power, and Mae always knew that power needed to be nurtured and tended. At times, that meant using meanness and ridicule, for power is fueled by respect, and many times, respect is fueled by fear.

It was a wonderful thing to watch her hold court—she would entwine her fingers as if trapping a baby bird that she deeply cared for, and then mid-conversation, she'd crush it with the wringing of her hands, then, checking herself in the closest reflection, would squint her eyes slightly and adjust her angle to her vain satisfaction. In a group Mae would launch into her act, her little insults and bossy gestures warning everyone within her reign that she could make or break you, but then privately, in a one on one meeting, she'd turn on the charm and act like your closest friend.

At a party once, Mae introduced me to some powerful pals, then whispered:

"You could slay all of these bozos." Her look was menacing, affirming to me the primal need for ruthlessness in the land of fantasy.

Mae continues to stare at me from the grassy lot, and once again softly waves to me. With each passing second, she gets older, her posture slacking, and her hair graying. Around her, the buildings of modern North Hollywood begin to grow back, rising up like in stop-motion photography. I see the years passing—orchards disappearing, wires ascending, noise increasing. I think of the apples, the note, the eggs, and the whirring drone noise.

I open my eyes to find that everything's normal again, though I do feel as if I have somewhat of a hangover. I'm back in my car, parked next to a Mattress Man and his truck. The driver's soft eyes calmly smile at me, which is comforting.

"I have a letter for you," he says.

Mae... why was Mae here? I think to myself.

"We did not bring anyone," he chuckles as if reading my thoughts.

"What's happening here?" I ask him.

"We just bring them. The messages." His firm tone is calming and disarming.

"You're Armando, right? You know Roberto... the big one, right?"

Armando just smiles, and nods his head in the affirmative. He looks real happy, almost carefree.

"Some will be easy—some will be hard. Here's the list," he says.

He hands me an envelope. The envelope is just like the one that came under my door, not parchment, but bearing a patina that brings musty, aged paper to mind.

"What should I do with this?" I gently press.

"You're to fix all six."

"Fix—fix what?" I press a tad harder as I sense this has taken a burdensome turn.

"Some will be easy—some will be hard," he repeats.

The whirring sound emanates from the truck, and I'm guessing it's a radio signal of sorts coming from within the truck. Armando checks something inside by the dashboard.

"You keep saying that pal, but what's easy and hard?" I tersely ask.

"I go now. You will only see one name at a time on the list. Look now for number one—it will be there. The rest will follow, and you'll fix them all—you must fix them all. If not..."

"If not, what?" I nervously inquire.

"I cannot tell you anymore. The only way you will learn is by following the list. Some will be easy—some

will be hard. Oh I forgot, here is your stake money...
your expenses."

Armando hands me six thousand dollars in one
hundred dollar bills. I am shocked and silently think,
Hallelujah.

"Hallelujah indeed, my friend," Armando says, as
if reading my thoughts once again. "You will need this
money—there's no work left in this town for you. There
will be more money, because this is your new job—
you're not a writer anymore."

"What the hell do you mean I'm not a writer anymore? What the hell are you talking about?"

Another time glitch and I'm driving again.

There are cars to the left and right. The traffic is
loud, and the light is quite intense. It's so bright that I
crave shade, like when you come out of the eye doctor
with dilated pupils. The morning mist has burned off
so I'm guessing it must be later in the morning, maybe
even closer to noon.

I pass a clock and indeed it is just about noon, and I
find it somewhat strange that I'm not more alarmed at
the loss of two whole hours. Next to me on my pristine
Dodge bench seat is the envelope the Mattress Man was
holding, and the six thousand in cash.

You'd think I would want to pull right over to see
what's in this letter that the Mattress Man gave to me,
however I seem to be driving with a hidden purpose,
one that I am resigned to and fine with.

I make a left at Moorpark Way and head east again

towards the lovely little town of Toluca Lake. I have a strong desire to visit one of my old haunts, a pub with a fairly long valley history. Many a marriage, deal, affair, divorce, and delicious burger have been cooked up inside its walls.

As I pull into the overcrowded parking lot that borders the rear alley, a valet parking attendant asks if I'm going in for lunch. After assuring him that I am, he gives me a ticket to park, then calmly smiles.

"I like your old car, it's a real nice old Dodge," the valet attendant says. "You know these cars ride better than any new car."

Then quite strangely, he puts his hand on my shoulder and softly says:

"Be very careful crossing the alley, my friend."

The attendant turns away and goes back to his crowded parking lot, then, just as I step across the alley, a low slung 1932 Ford hot rod roadster comes roaring around the corner speeding right towards me, very nearly running me down as it hits second gear. The driver adjusts his direction again, seemingly towards me, spinning his rear whitewall slicks on some sandy spots in the alley pavement.

I jump out of the way just in time and catch a glimpse of the driver. It's none other than the studio head Lawrence Fischer, my former boss and the host of those lavish Hollywood parties. He pays me no mind save for a quick emotionless look, followed by a phony but charming smile—one that makes me feel as if I should send him a thank-you card for not running me down.

As his roadster moves down the alley, I turn to thank the valet attendant for his prophetic warning, but find no one there. The entire parking lot is completely empty except for my old Dodge.

With each step towards the door, I swell more and more with a horrible sense of pending trouble, and right on cue, the remnants of the jagged light begin to bounce around my head once again. I close my eyes for a second and try to wash it out and away, when I notice the weeds on the sidewalk under my feet, just like the ones on Lankershim Boulevard by Jane's record store.

As I swing open the door upon entry, my whole world goes dark. I haven't blacked out because I can feel my feet walking forward onto the carpet in a space totally pitch and void of sound. I can't see it, but I know I am clutching the letter from the Mattress Man, and I can feel its significant presence in my hand.

Then from the darkness, I hear a voice.

"They chose you, Truman? I mean I knew this was coming, but you're the one? My God."

With near theatrical drama, a light clicks on above the person seated at the pitched black bar. If this were a Broadway production, I would expect to hear applause with the illumination and reveal of this character, but being that it's silent; it reminds me of a PBS studio no-audience-telecast of the same.

Asher Corrigan, the famous director, raises his

eyebrows, then his cocktail in a soft salute to my unexpected presence. Asher was introduced to me many years ago by Mae McLaughlin right before his first big movie *Murderous Thugs* came out. Since then, it's been one violent hit after another. Here, he sits awash in a sharp overhead light, which for him is not the most becoming of illuminations.

"I think you will find this is an easy one," Asher deeply and deftly vocalizes. "We had a spat. I felt bad—you felt bad. You got crap gigs, I got awesome ones," he says softly with a slight chuckle. "A human frailty—a human error. It needs to be righted."

His eyes scan the room pointlessly, knowing full well that no one else is here.

Indeed, a couple of years back, Asher Corrigan and I exchanged words late one evening, right where he sits at this surreal moment. At the time, I felt he was ridiculing me unjustly me over a silly trivial detail. He was chastising me for not knowing about a certain old actor. It was his way, a snobbish way, which I guess he felt entitled to. I was a little thin-skinned, and then from atop my pity pot, I lashed out. In my non-grata state, I reacted like a lame wounded bird pecking the hand that reached into my convalescent cardboard box.

The envelope, the one from the Mattress Man, vibrates in my hand. I carefully open it, and take a look inside. The first name is there by itself, right at the top of the letter.

Number One — Asher Corrigan.

The letters in his name seem to be buzzing—that's as best as I can explain it. They don't look as if they're written in ordinary ink. Numbers two through six have blank spaces after them. I think to myself, when someone loses their mind, is it as real as this is?

"It is happening, Tru, you aren't losing your mind. By the way, how's your friend Mae doing? I miss her so."

"Mae's dead, you know that, Asher. You were at her funeral."

Asher Corrigan nods and waves impatiently with the back of his hand as if to say, let's move on.

"Devils can be vanquished or released, Truman."

"Devils? Asher, you've had too much vodka," I tell him.

He then looks up at me as if he has just realized something.

"You don't know do you? I thought they would have told you—well, it just may be the language barrier. Anyway, I didn't know I was one until she… well, that's another story."

"So do we mean like mischievous bad-boy devils, or the hellfire dark-lord kind?

"Truman, this is not a joke, but yes, some of them will be very dark indeed."

"Okay if it's true, this dude Armando told me I had to fix all six. Is the word 'fix' the language barrier equivalent for 'vanquish'? And if that's true, isn't 'vanquish' the equivalent of 'kill'?"

"Fix, also means release, Truman."

"What do you mean by release?"

"Tru, we're not all fire-breathing horrors. There are many more good people that go off to their paradise by behaving a lot worse than I do. I felt stagnant, and I thought it would give me an edge in Hollywood, so I sort of went with it. Basically, I thought it was fashionable."

"You felt it would give you an edge?" I ask incredulously.

"Yeah, you know, the heavy godless debauchery, the stuff of the new American dream. Truman, do you know the amount of money that is spent on America's obsession with violence and death?"

Asher adjusts in his seat like he's ready to clear his mind. He takes a sip of his drink and taps the bar lightly with the tips of his manicured fingers.

"Americans love to see darkness played out for them, loud and proud," he says. "Me, I just wanted to hit the big time, so I figured out how to make the darkness attractive. New twists, hip characters, you know, the *artiste* thing. So, they took me on, got me going, you could say."

"They got you started in pictures?"

"Sort of... yes. Well, suffice it to say that they bent some minds, and gave me the edge I needed to make things more... desirable. Hey but that's old history, I've become a disappointment to them now. I figure since I have enough pictures under my belt, I shouldn't have to worry about the dark ones making or breaking me."

"So, what are you asking me, Asher?"

"I'm done, I just want a release—oh and to answer your question, 'release' means just about what it says. I just want to be let go from the darkness, so don't worry, you won't have to vanquish me. Hell, you don't seem like much of a vanquisher anyway."

He laughs, much to my annoyance, then continues:

"Truman, I've been going around making amends and straightening out my wreckage just so I can be released. However, you won't be able to do this for me until you're ready—and it's obvious that you're not. There are things you will need to experience, so I have a suggestion for you; listen to what the Mattress Men say, then act, clean and fast.

"Well, I'm off—I've said too much. I'll see you in about two or three months and hopefully then you'll be able to help me out." Asher takes a last sip of his vodka then closes. "Gotta go... see you around, Tru."

All of a sudden, there's some confusing pain on my right wrist as if I'm being pulled very fast by a large creature. I find myself seated at a table, and before me a beautiful but pale waitress is asking if I'd like any more iced tea. The room is crowded with diners. Trying to keep my composure, I go with it and simply reply:

"No."

"How was the turkey burger?" she adds as she bounces off to the kitchen.

My wrist still smarts and is slightly discolored. I wish I could have answered, but I've no recollection of having eaten it, except for the taste of onion in my mouth. The ghostly waitress brings the check and leaves it on the table.

I look around my old haunt and see all the nostalgic markers of romance, comedy, anger and sadness that framed my thirties. I'm a misty guy when it comes to old places, and this place holds a piece of me.

As if cued by the music supervisor from the very weird movie I seem to be starring in, Steely Dan's "Deacon Blues" begins to play on the jukebox. I pick up the check, look at it and notice there are no prices, tax or total. Scribbled in waitress handwriting with a smiley face below are the words:

Some will be easy—some will be hard.

Sleep will not come easy for this man tonight. Good sleep is usually reserved for the pure of conscience and healthy of mind, and being that I've seen a dead friend floating and at the same time been charged with eliminating six devils, there's a good chance I'll most likely be staring at my ugly popcorn-ceiling all damned night long.

CHAPTER 7

THE SANTA ANA WINDS

THE HIGH DESERT north of the valley heaved a hellish wind down into the town of Santa Clarita overnight. Santa Clarita, north of the San Fernando Valley and bordered by the Santa Susana Mountains, funneled on the demon visitor through its passes and canyons, bribing it with little souvenirs of mountain-dust and clay from its slopes in order to send it on its way. Pointing to the exit, it pushed the evil wind through its narrowed pass like a feverish breath through teeth, blasting it down onto the San Fernando Valley.

Seeking lower pressure for its mate, the wind shot out as if launched by a cannon—sand stinging the stucco and vinyl-sided homes, and etching minuscule Santa Ana signatures into the paint of the old cars in the poor streets, and the fancier ones in the better neighborhoods.

The wind against my windows nudges me awake, and in these sleep refreshed, rebooted moments of thought, I clearly see the formula for the swift, cruel passage of time. I suddenly realize that the years are bamboozled by their seasons, which in turn are distracted by the calendars of our chores, jobs, and responsibilities—which are rewarded and seduced by our wants, obsessions and pleasures that dull our senses, and under our slumber, another day, month, season and decade turn, leaving the tell-tale sign and sometimes sad memory of broken spirits, faded friendships, and never to be written novels.

There's nothing on the footboard. No hooded men with sickles standing over me. No Mae. My brain feels like it's floating on a calm river, with its most superficial thoughts stirring ripples on the surface.

Looking out the window I see a clear sky. The Santa Ana's have swept the June gloom away, but have replaced it with a higher chance of fire. The Santa Ana condition can dry out the valley in an hour, making grass and trees as brittle as kindling. Just one errant cigarette or spark could be catastrophic for the entire city, however I'll not add this worry to my shoulders today as I already have a full pack. As far as worries go, I think I'm doing very well with all this insanity. My personal measure of maturity has always been my ability to calm my worries and fears. In that lies self-confidence, perseverance, and the capacity for hope.

Another note whisks under my door.

No sound from outside, no whirring drone, just a

note, this time in a more modern type of envelope. The outside of the envelope bears the inscription:

To whom it Mae concern.

It has my attention.

Inside I find the contents of a slightly crumpled letter, one that appears to be written in my own hand, and dated exactly five years into the future. The address is in Manhattan, but it's one that I'm not familiar with. If I hadn't been through such bizarre happenings in the last twenty-four hours, I would assume that this is all a fairly good hoax.

> *Dear Me,*
>
> *Because of the circumstances you're in, you'll find this letter incredulous. In order to convince you that this letter is real, I'll say something to you that no one else could possibly know, hopefully then you'll take it seriously: Tina, Mary, Jean, Karen, Carol...*

I drop the letter. No one, but no one knows this strung together group of names. It's so silly, but those names come from a game I had partaken in during my seventh grade health education class. The teacher was trying to get his new classmates to remember each other's names. We took turns memorizing, and then calling out the names of everyone up and down the rows.

The first five people were Tina, Mary, Jean, Karen,

and Carol. These first names were a breeze to remember, and gave a running start of sorts for everyone playing the game. Saying those names rolled with a sharp rhythm off everyone's tongue and its alliteration has stayed with me all these years. I've never spoken about or related the story to anyone, so its inclusion in this letter is either verification of a bonafide communication from the future, or verification of pure delusional insanity. Since I don't like doctors or hospitals, I read on.

...I hope I have your attention dear self because I have to warn you that you may be experiencing some bizarre events in the next few days. I know you've already seen Mae floating and Asher Corrigan apologizing, but I'm not referring to that – that was easy, the next one is hard.

Grab hold tight and steel yourself for the task ahead of you. The Mattress Men are there to help, but not everyone is whom they seem to be. If I say more, I'll cause you even more trouble. Figuring this one out for yourself will save me as to my predicament now, and save you from the same for sure. I write this letter from the future to myself in the past so you can change it. If not, we die, right here where I am now – in your future. Remember, things are not always what they seem to be. That's the nature of these events. Stay strong, think of Dad and Uncle Frank.

Balls.

Yours,

You

Balls indeed, but it's too early for the Jack Daniel's bottle. Dad and Uncle Frank were certainly two guys I could reference if I ever wanted to buck-up and do what I had to do.

Uncle Frank was Dad's older brother and was in the first wave at Omaha Beach on D Day, June 6, 1944. He lost most of his hearing that day, and when he passed away a couple of years back, he still had some German shrapnel in his body. His was awarded all kinds of medals and his unit received a presidential citation for their actions that morning.

Dad was in Korea and then became a New York City policeman through the toughest riots and turmoil of the 1960s. They were two men of proven valor, and if they could get through what they needed to get through, then I could surely get through this.

The person that wrote the letter obviously knew of my two strange events yesterday, so either it's Asher screwing with me, or Mae is back from the dead (and screwing with me), or there are these Mattress Men named Roberto and Armando screwing with me, or me, entirely screwed in the head without anyone's help or hindrance.

Checking my voicemail, there's a message from

Jane Axton saying that my forty-five RPM record that I'd ordered had come in, and to please come by in the morning to pick it up.

"How about breakfast?" she adds.

I smile at the question, figuring there is no better time than in the middle of supernatural event to start an awesome romance.

As I begin to get ready, the other letter, the Six Devils letter from the Mattress Men, blows off my counter. Actually it looked like it flew off the counter, almost as if someone or something threw it. Noting my windows are firmly shut, I nervously walk over to give it the attention that it obviously demands.

I'm not very afraid of anything in this life, not afraid of anyone either. It's not a macho thing; it's another good quality that my father instilled in me as a young boy. He once told me:

"No one is any better or less than you. Always be kind to everyone—but never take any crap from anybody either."

It was a very American statement, and Dad was the consummate American. Those simple words seem to make me just a little braver than most people, not a tough guy, for I am surely not that, not a fighter at all, just a guy who won't put up with any elitist baloney. Those words were a gift from my father and have served as a great social neutralizer for me, for they bring powerful and supposedly frightening people down from lofty pedestals and always raise those less fortunate up to an equal footing.

I open the parchment envelope, and unfold the letter. Sure enough, his name is right there in the number two spot. It was the name I had entirely expected. Even though Dad taught me well, seeing it there on the paper sent a rotten little chill up my spine, not because the person was considered important, but because he's known to be so damned ruthless.

Number Two — Lawrence Fischer.

Lawrence Fischer, head of the studio, powerful, commanding, charming, yet nasty. He's the man who could have changed my life if he chose to, the man that nearly ran me over in the alley—the man that's ultimately responsible for my stolen scripts—the man I think they're asking me to kill.

He literally answers to no one, because everyone on the lot is in his employ in one way or another. If you say hello, most times you won't even rate a stiff glance. Fischer is pure cold business, being feared usually gets him what he wants, but there are also times when he can be quite charming and engaging. He knows his business backwards and forwards, and no one takes over a room or a meeting quite like Lawrence Fischer. He's just one of those people that you have to look at and listen to.

Fischer's not as young as Irving Thalberg was when Thalberg ruled over at Metro Goldwyn Mayer, but he's still only in his early forties and has been heading up the lot for around eight years now. Having majored in marketing at Harvard, then running his father's advertising agency for five years, he thought it time to come to Hollywood in order to take over the entertainment business. He actually wrote those words in his diary. Just like my old pal Cliff, Lawrence Fischer certainly had his own five-year plan, but his plan has taken him to the top of the heap.

Checking the time, I remember I have an appointment with Jane, and I begin to dress.

Levi's 1948 style jeans from their vintage line.

Calvin Klein black crew neck t-shirt.

Pendleton blue plaid "Board Shirt" worn open.

Coach belt, black.

Jeffrey Rush black boots.

Chanel Egoiste (non-platinum) cologne.

Checking myself in the mirror, I think I look decent, but I'm showing some age around the edges. I remember when I was a child, how I'd gaze in the mirror and try to imagine what I'd look like once I became a man.

The child was trying to see the future. Now, looking the other way, I can sometimes glimpse that child if only for the smallest moment. The boy I used to be is hiding somewhere behind those eyes, the ones that have seen maybe just a little too much.

When I saw my younger adult self yesterday during the strange event, it became all the more apparent to me at that precise moment, that the flesh is just a mere distraction— the very vessel of our disbelief.

CHAPTER 8
THE PESTILENCE OF EGO

O N MY WAY out, I paid my landlord with some of the cash that Armando gave me. He chuckled, and within that chuckle I found a warm welcome back into his good graces. I arrive at the record store to see Jane and take her up on her offer of breakfast, but am disappointed to find the store closed. Taped to the door is an envelope with my name on it. There's a note inside.

Hi, I figured you might be coming by this morning, but I had to fly. The prop master on the lot called and said he needed a whole bunch of forty-five RPM records, so I'm bringing them over to him.

I need an assistant (wink-wink), so I'll be leaving your name at the gate in case you have some time. Come meet me over at the prop department. Sorry about breakfast, but after I'm

*done, we'll have lunch at the commissary… my
treat!*

Hope you get this note,

Jane

My heart ran down the springboard and launched
aflutter in true Andy Hardy style. This girl has it all,
packed up into a tight fitting t-shirt and blue jeans. Yes,
Jane dear, I am interested in lunch, dinner or any meal
you care to share with me.

Jane did leave my name on the list at the studio
gate, and it gains me prompt admission. The guard tells
me to follow the peripheral road all the way over to the
prop department, which is on the east side of the lot.

The movie studio is a protected town, a walled
city, not unlike those near the fabled Black Forest of
Germany. Being that it's an encapsulated environment
with security at every portal and fantasy pouring from
every soundstage, it can sometimes seem like a selfish
version of Oz.

The rules of the real world rarely stray inside the
walls, so some of the people inside tend to develop a
surreal sense of detached and entitled importance.
These particular elitists seek special treatment for most
everything, and cite "cinematic immunity" whenever
they are asked to wait in line, practice what they preach,
or even stay at the scene of an accident. Here on the lot,
it seems to infect a good many, with the exception being

the lowest echelon of the screen accredited (e.g. the people who do most of the work).

When not dealing with its selfish people, I find the lot quite fascinating, and being a classic movie buff, I've spent many lunch hours walking around, perusing the old sound stages where so many of the classic productions were filmed.

Sometimes I'd give this haunted tour to anyone who cared to walk along and hear me blabber on about this old horror movie or that old mystery flick. However, most of the time it was usually just me, grabbing a hotdog and touring alone, which was okay, as those were some of my favorite private moments.

I drive my car past the commissary, and am amused at the many people standing, sitting and posing outside. The commissary's the social gathering place on the lot, but it also accurately represents this whole town. Hollywood is a show and tell affair where being seen with the right group of people is so very, very important. And speaking of important, sitting there outside alone at a table, I spy Asher Corrigan, and as if by radar, he looks up from his script and gives me a chilling wink, reminding me of my strange predicament.

I continue to drive on towards the prop department, and just as I'm about to turn onto the peripheral road, there's a stunningly beautiful young woman standing there at the roads edge with her thumb out, just plain old hitchhiking. She looks like one of the more feminine hot rod girls that hang out at some of the Burbank cruise-ins on Friday nights.

Everyone on this lot needs to clear security, so without any fear of anything untoward, I happily pull over for this roadside vision. I figure I can drop her where she needs to go, then cruise over to the prop house just in time to catch Jane.

Instead of getting into the passenger seat, she catwalks around the front of my long-hooded Dodge towards my side, swiveling her hips as if a director has yelled "action."

I roll down my old manual crank window and find myself staring down the barrel of a small loaded revolver—so much for the job security is doing.

"Mr. Lawrence Fischer wants to see you. Do I need this or will you be a nice little boy and give me lift with your old grandpa car?"

Ignoring the insult, all I can think of is; I must have been set up. Hopefully not by Jane, but then again, who else would've known I'd be driving along the peripheral road on the far side of the backlot? I've obviously been watching too many old movies, for I launch right into some lines from a film noir script.

"Get in, and put the pistol down, sweetheart."

As she walks back across the front of the car I have the strongest urge to hit the gas and mow her tight leather pants down, but then of course the papers would read:

Out of Work Writer Murders Promising Young Scientist.

I think past it, and let her in the car.

"You're one of his girlies?" I ask.

"Shut up and drive over to the office." She delivered her line slyly, pointing the unmistakable Smith & Wesson Model 36 snub-nosed revolver at my side.

"I'd drive better if you'd put that gun away. Besides, I'm supposed to see him… I want to."

"We know what you're all about, writer boy," she says. "We think you're going to suck as much at this, as you do at getting yourself any decent work."

I drive on for a few tense seconds before realizing that my young escort is playing it a little too thick for my tastes. To make that point, I jam on my old drum brakes and scuff up some of the un-swept sand and pebbles from the road.

She reacts like a scolded child, with a timid and abused look blooming red on her very young face.

"You know what you are? You're just a dopey head-shot, a silly little bimbo messenger. Listen up sweetie, it's you who'll do the shutting up, and while you're at it, stick that little pea shooter back up your ass."

This devil hunting wears well on me. I felt like Robert Mitchum delivering that line. I knew she wouldn't shoot me, for if she did, her hooker/actress life would be over.

She recoils, and lays the revolver down on her lap, and all at once my villainous passenger deflates into nothing more than a scolded, grounded, naughty over-made-up girl playing a cheap role. I actually feel sorry for her, and want to find where she lives and take her home, for she merely looks like a kid that's in way over her head.

I notice that she has bruises on her wrists and fore-arms, ones that looked like the marks of abuse. So now all of a sudden, I am tucked into the difficult place between anger and compassion, a place where words become quite sparse.

I remain quiet and circle back to her demanded destination. My guess is that Lawrence Fischer wants to move this along, so I figured I might as well get this over with and meet him face to face. Most likely he won't even be in, and I'll have plenty of time to meet up with Jane.

For the rest of the short ride, this young woman is quite still, and I had to resist the urge to tell her that it was all going to be okay.

I pull into the smaller private lot behind Fischer's office and we get out of the car. I turn around as if called, not by an audible voice, but by a strong silent one. Nothing is there except the water tower, with its presence emanating out from its center, presence thrust high up into the proud logo boldly displaying its fame. It always looks so regal and important, especially at night, when it basks in its own spotlights.

As we walk up to his bungalow, my hijacker retreats like one of the Munchkins, when the Wicked Witch of the north first appeared. I watch her scurry away, but notice that she regains her composure and model's swagger when she finally meshes with the bustling throng walking along on their way to the commissary.

I quickly put her out of my mind and pause to take a deep breath, then, remembering what Dad had told me (*no one is any better or less than you*); I steady myself for the meeting.

Opening his door, I notice it's a nice office with some original 1940s horror movie posters lining the walls. Their bright colors and fantastic logos once sweated over by forgotten artists so very long ago, give the room a needed anchor of patina in an otherwise modern space.

I notice the familiar names on the posters and highly doubt that Fischer has any real working knowledge or appreciation of these films, nor would he ever want to walk with me on my lunchtime tour to see where these actors, technicians and artists once worked—before he reigned here, before this was his lot.

As if from a horror film of his own, he's a frightful vision, calmly waiting there for me behind his desk. He smiles, and strangely, it feels very welcoming. It's a smile he'd developed at school before his promised advantage had been fully realized. It was meant for his professors and his competitors, and it still holds tremendous persuasive qualities. It's a siren's smile, full of promise, but I know better, for his smile serves as a warning of pending injury.

The alarm that I feel is deep-blue, and cold as a tomb, and it sends a damp chill into my bones, a chill as uncomfortable as a New York winter. I have a seat and look directly back at the man. If he thinks he will stare me into submission, he has another thought coming.

There have been several hypnotists in my past that have had their performances ruined, deeming me "not a good subject" whilst wiping egg from their faces. Here, I have to hold back from sticking my tongue out at him as he tightens his gaze, trying to tap it ever so slightly into the back of my head. I nearly mock him as his childish eyes light on fire and his silly cold grip clamps my legs.

Knowing that I can stop him at any time, I let him take me on a journey, entertaining his intense stare and relaxing my vision into a peaceful blur. The grip on my lower body grows as I pretend to have difficulty talking. I play drunk and watch in amusement as I shrewdly pass words from my mouth that come out in strange blobby shapes.

My tongue slowly pushes them past my teeth and lips. My perspective on everything turns like a leaf in the wind, leaving my body, and then quite rudely, someone else in the room interrupts my thoughts with moans and cries.

"Why are you doing this to me?" bounces off the walls, but I can't tell where it's coming from.

His gaze is now calm, and I've obviously won the battle. I take my victory lap across the room, bounding off the four walls in quick succession. Slowly, I fall back into the chair in front of his desk. The room brightens then goes silent with only the sound of wind in my ears. Suddenly I find that I am in a vast desert, with Fischer still sitting across from me, the smile having now turned diabolical, his face not unlike one from my worst childhood nightmares.

I am wondering now if he has tricked me, but then again, the answer supplied to a fool is always one that comes far too late. I look down to see my body whiten and begin to erode as if it were a pillar of sand being blown away by a hot wind. Question answered.

We stare at each other for what seems like hours. The sun goes down and the coyotes howl, high up in the radiating hills. His face looms large before me, not unlike my vision of Mae. I cannot move or say a thing, and don't even know if I still have a body—if I do, I'm surely unable to use it.

After a great amount of time, (it could have been days as my sense of time was as lost as my ability to ambulate), and with his face looking like a gazing vulture, he says his first words to me.

"Think back to your decisions in life, Truman," he instructs me calmly.

Knowing who is saying this upsets me. I resent every word this man has to say. With these words, the clouds roll over us like a muted string section, and then all of a sudden, we're once again in his office.

"You see, that right there is a thought that was influenced by one of your decisions—the decision to be equal—or to actually look down on someone like me.

Yes, I did hear you, and ordinarily I would never pay you any mind, but you've been chosen to vanquish me. Unlike that rat, Asher... I don't want a release." He is amused by his last words.

"Vanquish isn't as campy a deed as it is in one of these vampire movies," he says, pointing to the posters on the walls. "You'd have to kill me—blow my damned brains out, and quite frankly you don't have the balls."

At this point, I couldn't disagree with the man, for even if I had that girl's loaded revolver in my hands right now, I'd never be able to pull the trigger.

"You see, Truman, our business isn't fire and brimstone now—it's bad deals, and broken hearts. Lost adults who never grow up and forever dream of stardom, wasted careers and lives that could have been, but never were.

"A man comes out to California, leaves behind his Daisy Jane in Ohio, and the three kids that they never had. Daisy Jane gets a job as a cocktail waitress, becomes a drunk, gets fat, old and never marries. Their kids could have been scientists, or excellent small-town doctors that could have saved other children—that never were born as well, to the actress or the singer that was foolish enough to hope beyond the high school stage.

"Here's one," he says as he picks up a headshot of a lovely young girl. "She became a model, who thought she could act, who'll start doing coke, and will be murdered in North Hollywood, in just about two years. Worse yet, if I give her just one little role, she'll live on desperately looking for the next big job and will grow old in my funny little business."

His desk is filled with many eight-by-ten head-shots and resumes. Usually these calling cards offer the best smile or the sexiest look from the entertainer in the photo. Then with an eerie twist of reality, all of the smiling and sexy faces begin to age into the faces of unhappy and tortured older people. Some of the pho-tos on his desk begin crying and sobbing—then Fischer smiles that smile again.

"Ours is not fire, horns and pitchforks, ours is har-vesting the pestilence of ego. It'd be easy if you came here looking for and finding a pointy tail and fangs. There are no wild eyes, no long fingernails, no death ray. I'm not one of these characters that you love in these old horror film posters. The only evidence of my work, are these headshots, these scripts."

He then throws a pile of each into the trash bin next to his desk.

"There—those poor souls just lost twenty years off their lives. They're happy enough to be told by their agents that they had pictures or scripts on my desk—I'll trash them, but they'll still wait forever to be famous, trying again and again, reciting their self-empowering slogans that they put on their refrigerators. No one will ever tell them it's over, and they won't figure it out themselves, they'll just keep thinking positive thoughts.

"Each and every month they're harvested in to me by the thousands from the idol shows, magazines and movies. We start them off earlier and earlier now too. Truman, do you know how many third graders tell their teachers that they want to be famous? Every small child these days wants to be a singer or dancer, or just about anything else that will bring them fame. No more astronauts, no more explorers, no more presidents. And with each and every rare one we let through to fame and fortune, a hundred thousand more lost souls will make the decision, 'If they can do it, so can I.' So you see, Truman, my business blooms exponentially."

Holding up another photograph, of a young man, playing guitar, he adds:

"Ever see how many music stores cater to all those rotten rock bands that think they'll be the next big thing? It's a billion dollar industry. We feed the dream that turns into a nightmare. Our scientists and engineers are few and far between, with most of those jobs going to foreigners who aren't obsessed with me making them famous. That's my work Mr. Morrow... I collect their little souls."

I could do nothing but listen. He had me, at least as far as my undivided attention went.

"I'm as plain as a monster in a church, but most don't see it. I'm as inconspicuous as a wild boar, but have melded into the twenty-first century American wallpaper. You figured it out, Truman—you see the degradation, that's why you were chosen. Yes, you've wasted a good part of your life, but I paid you for your ideas, and… stole a few." He bursts out with a sick laugh.

"We almost had you believing—one more job, one more job, but let me show you Truman, what'll happen if you continue on your little game."

As his words are trailing off, I feel myself moving backward and forward, as if I'm on a violent carnival ride with a sick feeling developing in my stomach. I shut my eyes and wait for it to be over. As it subsides, I open them to find myself outside of his office, looking into his window.

There she was on his desk, face down—her platinum hair hanging over the edge and her beautiful arms gripping the sides. Her clothes are strewn about the floor, and her headshot is lying along side of a mirror— a mirror with white powder on it.

Fischer and another man are smiling and sweating as they ravage her, moaning and breathing in a raunchy, upsetting fashion. She attempts to reach for the lines of powder, but her arm is pulled behind her back in a sadistic manner by one of the two men having their way with her. The other man pulls her hair wrenching her head back, and for the first time I can see this woman's face.

The illness comes back upon my body when I realize this poor woman is indeed my dear friend Sherry. As I attempt to run around towards the office door with the intention of stopping them, my eyes are forced closed, and the sickening centrifugal force begins once again.

I open my eyes this time to find myself hovering over the main floor of a vast, dingy, monochromatic corporate office, looking at a man who is balding, over-weight, wearing a phone headset in a small cubicle. He is obviously selling insurance or service contracts and looks just about as miserable as you could get, as though his world has been utterly destroyed with the shattered remains glued squarely atop his shoulders.

I feel so very sorry for him that it takes me a few seconds to realize this miserable wretched older man is myself. There are photos on his cubicle wall, photos of younger happier days, with friends, with money—with Sherry.

Again, I'm whisked away from there to a grave-yard where a priest is praying with several others at a gravesite. Sherry's family is there and so am I, and I watch as her mother hands me a small book. It didn't take any Sherlockian powers to deduce whose burial it was. With that, I look down at my hands, move them, bend my knees a little, and blink. I'm whole again, standing in his office.

"How do you like your future, Truman? Well most of it is future anyway. We've already had the bitch, that part was a rewind. She's going to be a *big* star."

He turns off the sarcasm then adds:

"My hat is off to you, most men would be a puddle on the floor right now, begging for the funny wagon.

You're merely pale... very good. It's such a shame that you won't help us and join our side, but that's for another time. The issue is the game, and the game is very much on.

"Your armor is that you think of me as your equal, don't you? That sir is impressive. I think your dad taught you that, right? Oh, yes, during that little show you were screaming out for your daddy... that was the only real pathetic part. Truman, you do know that I tried to kill you in the alleyway behind that pub, just as a test. It's true—I can't hurt you yet."

I remain emotionless in front of him when I actually want to jump up and down and scream, "Why me?"

"Oh, I see you haven't been fully briefed as yet. No matter, I can't take advantage of your ignorance yet. However, merely being chosen will not make you successful, especially against me. Truman, you'll come to find that I am truly unstoppable."

He actually just challenged me in a schoolyard sort of way, and that gives me a thin sliver of hope. It's the first sign of weakness that my newly christened warrior brain has noticed in this fiend. What's so odd is that as much as I despise him, and even with the horrors that he has shown me, I've no desire to kill the man.

"You don't even hate me do you? Some devil hunter!"

With a laugh, he looks to the door.

"Gentlemen," he says to his team of quietly

assembled security guards, "Mr. Morrow needs to find the exit gate."

As I am roughly led out of his office across the lot past the watchful eye of the water tower and Jane's Axton's parked '39 Lincoln, I noticed a plainly dressed forty-something man, more Mid-Western than Southern California looking, pleading with the guard for a visitor's pass onto the lot.

"Come on fella, my niece wants me to personally deliver this bottle of wine to Mr. Fischer. He sent her this note; 'If ever you should have any trouble getting onto the lot, just show them this. — L. Fischer.'"

He then shows the note to the guard.

"Mr. Fischer gave this note to your niece, certainly not to you, Mr. Ron Carson."

Looking as if he's seen this kind of trick before, the security supervisor coldly points the man to the exit in a lazy matter of fact way.

"The letter wasn't just for my niece, jackass, it was for my daughter and niece. And you know just who I'm talking about, don't you?"

The guard nonchalantly turns to his underling and quietly says:

"Call P.D."

The man gives up, gets back in his car and makes a u-turn away from the gate disappearing into afternoon traffic.

As Fischer's guards walk me to my car, I notice a mattress truck trailing blue smoke, passing by the studio, seemingly following after the man that just left. Starting my car, I also see Jane leaving the gate in her '39 Lincoln. Again, I can't help but wonder if she's lured me here, or if she's just angry with me for standing her up, but either way, I'm far too weak for all this drama—I need to go home to reflect on what Fischer has told me.

With his uniformed goons still watching me impatiently, I stomp the gas on my exit, giving them a nice taste of some early sixties Dodge tire smoke.

CHAPTER 9

THE LADY IN THE PHOTOGRAPH

WHEN EASTERNERS COME to Los Angeles to live, immediately we're at odds with our feelings. Surely the tried and true Eastern towns and cities of our forefathers, with their old bridges, tall buildings, and world class museums, are more important than this overblown string of hamburger joints, stretching from the peaceful coast, past the Hollywood sign, then thinly evaporating into the buzzing desert.

Surely the land of my lineage and toiling generations holds more importance in my soul than the stunning palm trees silhouetted against the sunset. Indubitably, Wagner, from tenth-row-center at The Met, cannot compete with the Friday night cruise-in at Bob's Big Boy in Burbank—can it?

Unless we are very careful about our wants and needs and are absolutely sure whom we are as a person, comfortable in our feelings and confident that our feet are where they should be, we risk being lost between two coasts—holding onto our snobbish ridicule of the West, but at the same time showing a disdain for our old East Coast ways.

For over fourteen years, I've tried to make peace with my old self—taking the hand of the carefree peaceful Westerner, leaving behind the serious, broody, and cultured New Yorker, just to go visit a few hamburger joints in my old '64.

In my heart, as much as I feel a disdain for this land, I hold deep veins of love for its simple attractiveness, and plain Western magic. In such, it's a demonstration of how I am truly a man at odds with himself—a man indeed lost between two coasts.

Even though I now pine for the comfort of a fireplace and a cold winter, once I leave here, once I leave the old cars, the cruise-ins, the studios, the perfumed air, I know I will miss it all so very dearly, forever lost, forever standing in my dreams in the middle of the nation, looking back and forth, east then west, while years tick away, friends grow old, and opportunities pack up and wander off.

Lately, there's a spark of hope, a bridge in my yearning for East Coast grounding and Western freedom. The bridge is the lovely Jane Axton.

After digesting my disturbing meeting with Fischer, I've come to the conclusion that Jane has nothing to do with any of this, for the simple reason that if she wanted to do me in, she would've had ample opportunity to do so. It's hard for me to admit such dependence, but I'm growing very attached to her. She could very well hold the link between my reality and this departure from it, and being that she is of the West; light, free, beautiful and bright, she mixes my two coasts together and soothes my nerves like a strong New York cocktail in the soft Malibu twilight.

I want to tell her about what's going on, I want to include her in the events that have rocked the core of my life. I just don't know where to start, and I'm so afraid that she'll run away—any sane person would.

Once again, the Santa Ana winds have died down to a mere hellish breeze and the summer moves on. The heat swirls, like in a giant convection oven, scorching the Southland's roads, clay, dust and people. I venture out of my air-conditioning and amble up the weedy, dusty Lankershim Boulevard past the aging coffee shops and smelly used clothing stores arriving at Trader John's record shop.

I see Jane and begin my thumbing through the stacks.

I watch her with another customer—Jane Axton is such a stunningly beautiful woman. She's fun, yet serious, has a gorgeous face that needs no makeup, a youthful way that leaves most women insecure, and an awesome body that leaves most men wanting. From this angle, you can't even tell that she's blind in one eye. In fact, sometimes I even forget which eye it is.

Jane's an amateur valley historian, with numerous amounts of old photos on the walls around her shop, and once again, she touches my soul with her appreciation for the old town that's long gone.

There are pictures of the old El Portal Theater, the Red Car line and the beautiful orchards that decorated the area we now know as North Hollywood. One photo is a postcard with a bird's eye view of the surrounding streets. *"Greetings from Lankershim"* is printed on top in a handsome 1920s typeface. If you look closely at the photo, in the distance, you can see the long stretches of groves, lonely dirt roads and empty spaces.

This valley must have been so beautiful back then, but the dirt roads have grown into four-lane boulevards, and the orchards are long gone. Jane's a romantic, because she can still see the beauty of the valley under the layers of concrete, swirls of graffiti and the curtain of lost time. That's part of my attraction to her—as I think we're both looking for something that could never, ever exist again.

Weeks have gone by since the strange demon interludes began, but since my encounter with Lawrence Fischer, there have been no significant incidents, except for the fact that I see mattress trucks most every time I leave my home. I see them on freeways, boulevards, and lurking down alleys. I wave to them, and they wave back. Sometimes it's big Roberto, Armando, or others that I haven't been introduced to yet—one other time I could swear there was no one driving.

I don't think this spiritual upheaval (if that's what it is), is over by any means; it's just that I'm feeling different about it. My acceptance of seeing supernatural beings is almost as puzzling to me as the beings themselves. I feel like a character in a ghost story, one where the mortal is not afraid of the spirit at all. I guess you could say that life feels just about as natural as supernatural can get.

In this strange time, Jane has been my anchor to reality and humanity, and we've seen each other more than a few times. A couple of weeks ago we went dancing, and I could have sworn that Jane had taken lessons from Fred Astaire himself.

She lit up that dance floor, and since I am just short of two left feet, I was totally accepting of anyone that wanted to cut in. With the way Jane Axton looked that night, there were many that seized that opportunity, and the poor dear had to fight to take a breather.

Another day we decided to go touring around the valley, just to see the remnants of the old days. We sought out signs of history in its buildings and streets, what came before, who built it, who owned it... essentially where we of the valley came from.

"That's the old radio station."

We stopped by the side of the road in front of a valley landmark. Jane pointed to the wonderful old building on Van Nuys Boulevard, a building that sat in a gigantic, wide-open parcel of land, with thin, high antennas surrounding it.

"Isn't it beautiful?"

"It is," I said, and I meant it. That old art deco radio station in the middle of the empty expanse seemed to defy all the laws of commerce and finance, for it was the only building in the valley that staked out such a wide claim in its congested valuable landscape.

"I used to listen to some great programs that came from here," she said. She seemed a bit misty looking at the place, then, snapped out of it by asking, "How about some lunch?"

Jane was great at giving subtle direction to any meeting, almost like she had persuasive mind power over me. But then again, I would pretty much do any-thing for this beautiful woman. So off we went to a fine lunch, where we shared long romantic stares, interspersed by polite little bites of our sandwiches. Our feet met under the table, and she put both of hers around my ankle, then our hands followed suit and played mischievously, touching each other's palms lightly.

I leaned across the table and kissed her, almost for-getting where we were. Then right on cue, the waitress brought our check, and with it, us back to earth, break-ing the spell.

Another time I returned the favor and took her on my little backlot tour, pointing out all of the historic spots from the earlier days in film. Not to my surprise, Jane spoke mournfully about the advent of sound and the changeover that took its toll on so many in the acting profession. At times, she seemed somewhat shaken by the images and events I described as if she had a personal stake in every story. Jane is a deep, old soul, and just by holding her hand, I feel wonderful things.

There aren't many people I know who look back at the history of the valley, for this is the land of no rear-view mirror. Jane's mirror works just fine, and she wears the wisdom of a person lost in time quite well. Normally you'd expect this from a librarian or an elderly shut-in, certainly not from someone as vibrant and redhead-sexy as she is.

Her customer leaves with a tinkling of the doors hanging bell, and she comes over to me, brushes some fuzz off my shirt, and fixes my poorly rolled sleeve.

"You're very nice, Truman... it doesn't need to be a big event for good character to reveal itself. It can be a tiny event. You paid me fifteen dollars for that record I ordered for you, and I know it wasn't the one you wanted. I ordered the wrong version. You wanted the Nat King Cole—I got the Natalie Cole."

"Some people would say that I'm a sap—a people pleaser," I tell her.

"You're not. You're a good man—I know."

"Well, I'd buy just about anything you'd sell me," I say as I inch closer to her, brushing her t-shirt playfully like she did mine. "On second thought Ms. Axton, I'll barter for the Natalie Cole record by offering in return, say... dinner for two, for the next five or six Saturday nights?"

She gently smiles and touches my hand almost as if to stop my playful touches that are getting a little too close to her chest. If I'm not mistaken, I see a trace of emotion well up in her face. It could be shyness, or it could be regret.

"Thanks, Tru."

Then, reversing whatever she was thinking, she moves close and kisses me with great passion. When a woman like this kisses you, the world goes silent for a minute. This is what kissing's all about—not just a pressing of the lips, but a stirring communication between two souls, through parts of the human body that speak, eat, and smile. Her lips, so very soft, full and delicious, actually bring me close to an old fashioned swoon.

When I recover my senses, I think another silly, weak thought:

I haven't had a kiss like this since... Erica. My God, this woman could be my savior.

We make plans for this Saturday night, and say our goodbyes, just as another customer comes in the door. As I'm leaving, I notice some more vintage black and white photographs on the wall, just behind the front counter.

There's one certain old photograph that catches my attention, it has the faded words, *Come To Lankershim*, written on the yellowed scalloped-edged border. The photo appears to have been taken a very long time ago, up by the old town square.

In the photo, there's a woman in the old rose garden with an eye patch on—there are three rose bushes on each side of her. She is a very serious looking and attractive woman.

CHAPTER 10

IDEA MAN

Dear Diary,

At this time, there is a disturbance in the bland benevolence of Truman's condo association, and I am knee-deep in it. Mindy, the president of the association is a mutual friend and came to me asking if I've had any dealings with one of the residents, Mr. Vince Shank. She knew I had, but she couldn't ask me directly, and had to pose it in a cloak. Mindy mentioned that there'd been some suspicious activity and traffic going to and from Vince's townhouse. I lied to her, I told her I haven't heard or noticed any strange activity around the neighborhood, and that I really didn't know Vince Shank.

Fischer better give me this part, although I am starting to think that he never will. Hell hath no fury like an actress without any hope.

– Sherry Cleveland

*

Failure in life makes you gun-shy of your future endeavors, and can leave a poisonous self-fulfilling prophecy in its wake. At times, our valiant querulous efforts can become the seed of embitterment, and our grasping at lost youth becomes the entrance ticket to our old age.

Los Angeles is a siren—she calls to the curious, the desperate, the hopeful, the lost and the wicked. The steady, ever ready sun seems to calm all wakes of guilt and mollifies all introspective sifting, allowing many to pass into marginal or bad behavior. I have been selected to wage a battle against some rotten people, but at times it feels so very overwhelming. In this day and age, at any given moment, I can open up my front door and come face to face with some of the world's worst scum.

Vince Shank sits by our association's pool most every early evening, with his mirrored sunglasses hiding the beadiest of eyes over a mouth pursed in the sleaziest of smirks. He's lived here for years, and no one really has anything good to say about him. He doesn't keep up the exterior of his unit (a big no-no with the condo board), and isn't particularly friendly towards anyone.

I hear he works for one of the big video game companies out in Santa Monica—that's a commute I wouldn't want for anything. To get from the valley to Santa Monica requires that you travel west on the Ventura Freeway, and then south on the San Diego

Freeway, where it's quite common to find bumper-to-bumper traffic at two a.m. If there's one excuse as to why his place looks so bad, it may be that Vince Shank is perpetually commuting.

He's most assuredly a partier as his face bears a roadmap of his not so good times, and that lifestyle makes him look older than his years. He's always disappearing into his place every twenty minutes or so when he's poolside, and then his demeanor will shoot high and then fall low, excited then morose. I have seen this type of behavior before, more times then I'd like to admit to.

Vince and I have been introduced about twenty times at different condo parties and events, and each and every time we meet he hands me his business card and says, "Nice to meet you."

When I did engage in conversation with him, I noticed that he had a nervous habit of checking his watch about every minute or so as if he were timing the sheer agony of our conversation together. Whenever I've had female guests at the pool, they've always remarked how Vince gave them the creeps. When he's asked, "how are you?" he responds with a terse "good," without even a thought of returning the nicety.

Our condo president has told me that this moribund man is affectionately known as "Dr. Addictive" at his company. He supposedly specializes in adding just the right amount of challenge in order to make the video games extra poisonous and all consuming to the small children, teens and adults that waste years of their lives playing them. I'm told he's an expert at it, with a job description so nebulous, his business card merely says:

Vince Shank – Idea Person.

Every once in a while, someone comes along in your life that becomes a mile marker of sorts, the summation of a string of people that you have met or dealt with up to that particular point. This person can represent good experiences or bad. So, after having had some really rotten interactions with Mr. Vince Shank, I can announce that I have chosen him as the definitive, central casting, Hollywood scumbag.

Lately, strange comings and goings by some odd folks have darkened our usually serene condo complex. Most days, groups of two or maybe three people enter his place, then leave just five minutes later. This happens several times a day.

There've been a few late-night disturbances also, like the time these two young girls ran screaming from his place. Well, one was screaming, the other was trying to get her to return.

"Do you want the part or not?" she yelled at her friend.

Upon hearing the commotion, I pulled myself away from my deep friendship with the television and poked outside. The recipient of the not so veiled ultimatum was clearly beside herself with fear and anger. I stage-whispered across the cemented courtyard:

"Can I help you ladies, is everything okay?'

They both stared at me with blank expressions, looking like two lost puppies that had been beaten and kicked by a horrific owner. Seeing me, they quietly turned and walked back into Shank's place. I heard nothing more from those two young women again.

Usually, I'd never have anything to do with a creep like Vince Shank. Hollywood is full of them, so I've had a lot of practice in ignoring their kind. Vince Shank sums up all the bloodsuckers, takers, users, and abusers this town has to offer and is truly an ugly man inside and out.

When he needs something, Shank can turn on the penny cheap charm, almost as if you could hear his thoughts ticking through the process of planning his manipulation of others for his gain. Even his trivial needs around our complex are achieved with the phoniest of deliveries.

"Hello, Truman, how are you? I'm Vince Shank."

"Yeah I know, Vince. We've met several times."

"Really? Mindy tells me you are quite the repairman. I hear you can fix almost anything. My kitchen faucet has developed a bit of a leak."

All of a sudden the man knows who I am and becomes bright and sunny. I was so ingratiated that I loaned him some tools that he never, ever returned.

The next time he came over for a similar request, I told him I had a producer on the line, and that I'd have to get back to him a little later. (That's more Hollywood speak for "Hell no, you jackass.") Since then, he's been a sneering freak that practically hisses whenever we lock eyes around our complex.

The most disturbing thing about Vince Shank is the fact that my condo president Mindy said she saw Sherry going in and out of his place several times in the last few weeks.

"Isn't she a friend of yours?" Mindy inquired.

Mindy might as well be the president of the maternal order of shit stirrers—she damned well knows that Sherry and I are friends.

Just a few days ago, I was out for a run early one morning and there he was, Vince Shank, dressed all in black from head to toe in what looked to be like Sunset Boulevard clubbing clothes. I found the contrast between his dark attire and pale pockmarked face to be quite stark and upsetting that early in the morning, but the fact that he was exiting Sherry's building, is what actually made me so very sick indeed.

It didn't take much of a leap in imagination to see that he'd spent the night at her place. He saw that I noticed him, and said:

"Just came over to loan her my tool."

It took all my strength not to fetch my car and run his ass over several times.

At that very moment, Sherry had used up the last of her chances with me, and the last romantic string that linked us was completely severed. Right then, I knew Sherry was truly lost, and when Shank was finally out of sight, a wrath swelled up in me like I'd never felt before.

It was a strange feeling when I prayed to whomever would listen, for his swift demise.

*

Dear Diary, July 1

A few years back, he came and went in the first summer we were here, taking care of my cats when I would drift back and forth across the country, not knowing whether I was an Easterner or a Westerner. I'd come back and smell his cologne that lingered from his recent visit. It hid in the lonely corners of my apartment and softly welcomed me home each time. He always left me a fresh quart of milk in my 'fridge for my morning coffee. This kind of thoughtfulness is a rare commodity in a man these days.

I came out on a mission to be something wonderful, but became something very ill indeed. At times I think I tried too hard to love him and ultimately pushed him away, like when trying to savor the remnants of his cologne – for after too many deep, searching breaths, the fragrance would just vanish.

The cocaine started as a lark when Lawrence Fischer introduced me to Vince Shank. He said that Vince would get me voiceover work on his video games. I've never even got so much as an audition, although after a while, I began playing an ugly role in his condo, giving myself to him in return for a fix or two. I've joined the team, along with Vince, led by Fischer. It's too late to save my poor self, but maybe not too late to stop one of them.

What they didn't count on was my love for him — my deep love for Truman. They're looking for a woman to kill him, but I'll never do it.

— Sherry Cleveland

CHAPTER 11

THE EXPECTATIONS OF THE FALLEN

I STOP INTO A local drinking establishment that I've frequented over the last few months. I start the evening by apologizing across the bar to a beautiful bartender for the behavior of a guy I'd hung out with last week. Drink after drink he proceeded to say the stupidest booze-laden things to this attractive young lady.

Although I didn't say anything, it was embarrassing and uncomfortable, and I felt the need to clear the air. This guy wasn't a real friend, he was just one of those low substance, proximity based acquaintances that can only exist in a dark place with a jukebox. When you take these kinds of relationships out into the light of day, they shrivel up and float off without any knowledge of a last name.

On the subject of friends, Los Angeles has been peeling away mine one by one. The phonies went first, then the half phonies, then good acquaintances, and now the final blow—Sherry.

Knowing she was with Vince Shank last night shook me deep and rocked my faith in a higher power that really should be metering some kind of fairness somewhere in this mess. It's enough to make me want to leave this town, but then again, where would I go? Certainly not back East.

On my most recent trip back, I tried to initiate a gathering of old pals, but only two old buddies joined me for the homecoming. There were promises from others, but they never came. When my father passed away a few months after that, I was back East again, and those same two old friends were the only ones that bothered to come to the wake. So many others were informed; all recipients of my condolences for their losses over the years, but none of them had the decency to call or even send a card.

I'm not a vengeful man, however, these former friends have been removed from my life forever. At my age, time is a precious commodity, so I no longer make time for people who just aren't worth one second of it.

"Oh that's okay your buddy wasn't that bad, I've already forgotten about it," the beautiful bartender says, with her stiff lips and rapid eye blinks betraying her guilt by association opinion of me. She then coldly pours me a Jack Daniel's on the rocks, and turns her back. I finish my drink a little lower down the "regular" ladder than I had previously thought I'd ascended to.

I have spent a good amount of money here over the last few months fully knowing the expectations of the fallen might cause me to snivel and stoop as opposed to being treated at the level of my former station. In this town, it's easy to claw your way down into a ditch of mistakes with just a few stupid moves. In all truth, this visit was just an excuse to get the guts up to go see the lovely Jane Axton. Like some of those worthless friends back East, this bar isn't worth the trouble, so, it too is history for the likes of me. Say goodbye, Mr. Daniel—adieu sweetheart.

Just the fact that I am taking the time to do normal things like date, shop, go to the dentist, or the motor vehicle bureau in the midst of this strange interlude, is quite bizarre to me and at times makes me laugh. It is hard to explain, but the juxtaposition of everyday events to supernatural ones is quite peculiar, especially when I still need my clothes washed, teeth brushed, nails clipped etc. It's just so anti-climactic and undistinguished for a supernatural kind of guy.

If this were a movie, I don't think the normal stuff would be included in the script. My character would probably be whisked away by the CIA or NASA, floating out in space, or in a cuckoo house. However, here I am washing socks, watering my flowers on the balcony and pursuing my latest passion: Jane Axton.

Sweet Jane in blue jeans. Sweet Jane with the red hair. Sweet Jane with the fullest lips, over the sweetest smile you've ever seen. This woman is getting under my skin, and just today I suppressed the urge to call her at least five or six times.

Usually when I feel like this about a woman, I know it's either obsession or a diversion from something else I'm supposed to be doing. Obsession usually brings worry and ill behavior, but I have no ill feelings or insecurities towards Jane, and will take what comes, even if nothing comes out of it.

I guess that means my interest in her is healthy. So combining my true feelings towards her with the wonderful oddity of her shop—no offense dear Mattress Men, but we need a pause—it's all about Jane right now.

Tonight is July 3. My old car has no air conditioning, so I drive with my windows open, and the cool night air of the valley mixes with the wonderful old smell of an all-original vintage-cloth, front bench seat. I hear the impatient youngsters and childish adults shooting off their firecrackers in the distance, obviously being unable to wait until tomorrow night.

Some of the patriotic revelers must be close by as the pops and flashes are bouncing off and illuminating the tall palm and eucalyptus trees on the next block. Unfortunately, during the rest of the year, when you hear pops in the valley it usually means gunfire. Tonight, I am unconcerned because it sounds soothing to my ears, like lost music from my youth, back when the Fourth of July really meant a whole lot to me.

I arrive at Jane's duplex apartment building. It's an older but charming place, sporting a white stucco exterior trimmed in blue, with vintage wood shutters and a wonderful old rough grained wood door. The porthole type window that accompanies the entrance-way was a bold design statement in its day, and adds a visual focal point to the plain white exterior of the home.

Just as I'm about to press her vintage round door-bell, the world around me begins to hum, and I feel a weighty ominous presence swarm up from behind. It feels like a middle ear infection, the kind that serves up a low frequency buzz and a dizzying headache.

My hand is unable to move forward towards the doorbell, and against my will I am slowly pivoted back towards the street. The slowness of the turn is machine-like and very much involuntary. The skies grow dark, and the valley becomes unnaturally silent, with no sounds from the revelers, birds, cars, or wind. Gone is the omnipresent drone of freeway traffic noise.

Off in the distance, I hear the unmistakable sound of a lone, open-piped, flathead Ford engine. I can't see it, but I'd know that sound anywhere, echoing against the curtain of dusk. It's the sound that could only emanate from a hot rod—a hot rod just like Lawrence Fischer's. I hear this car pull up at the curb, but see nothing, and then hear it peel off and speed away.

Slowly appearing from nothing at the curb is the disturbing sight of my evil neighbor, Vince Shank. He's standing there on the sidewalk completely still, like an old movie vampire, gazing at me with a penetrating horrible stare. His face appears to be glowing from within and stands out pronounced by the quickening blackness. I am literally paralyzed as he rises up slightly, then quickly floats to my side.

"She's ours you piece of shit—we'll kill you, or she'll fucking kill you," he whispers so very sickly in my ear.

With the tail end of the violent phrase, my finger is pressing Jane's doorbell and all's as it was, except for the fact that I am dripping wet with cold perspiration.

"Tru, you look white as a sheet," Jane says softly as she sees me. "You okay?"

I am reticent to tell her what has happened for two reasons, first, she might call the crazy house, and second, I am erring on the side of heeding Vince Shank's warning.

"What's that in your hand?" she says as she turns to walk back to her kitchen.

I step into her place and look down and see that I am holding the Six Devils letter from the Mattress Men—the letter that keeps reappearing. I unfold it, and am not surprised by the name that's listed, but very relieved to see whose isn't.

Number Three — Vince Shank.

A mechanical drone emanates from outside. I look out the window just in time to see a mattress truck pulling away from the curb.

Dear Diary, July 3

Detective Vega from the LAPD contacted me this morning. He tried to scare me with a drug possession charge, and then kept asking about Vince Shank. He even had some questions about Lawrence Fischer, and then requested I take a trip down to Parker Center. Detective Vega was kind to me, but he most certainly had an agenda.

He showed me a photo of two very pretty young actresses, maybe eighteen or nineteen years old. He told me that one had died, and then asked me if I'd ever seen her over at Vince Shank's house. I told him I hadn't, but after coming home and thinking about it, I remembered that I had seen her before, somewhere around six months ago.

It was a sordid memory, for she was one of my kind — a party girl. I'm fairly sure it was her that I partied with in a most unusual way. Frankly, it was more of a performance than a party.

Detective Vega said he wanted me to stay away from Shank, he told me my life was in danger. Then something very strange happened; he took me by the shoulders and looked very deeply into my eyes. I tried to avert my glance, but couldn't. He had the most peaceful gaze I'd ever seen.

– Sherry Cleveland

CHAPTER 12
FISCHER'S GIRL

(Based on an interview of Ron Carson's niece, Courtney, by Detective Vega LAPD, written one year later. Inserted here for continuity.)

COURTNEY CARSON BORE the bruises of abuse from the hands of a very nasty man.

What Lawrence Fischer and his friend did to her last night went far beyond sex. They were sadistic, vile and brutal to her, and they loved every minute of it. There were times when she thought she would run, but Fischer's diseased grip tightened day after day and like any abused person, she felt trapped.

Just two short years ago, she left home with her cousin, abandoning her loving uncle and adopted father, who had taken her in when she was just nine years old. She and her cousin Janice left him behind that day on the lot—the same day that they came to meet Lawrence Fischer.

Uncle Ron raised his niece and his daughter Janice to the best of his ability. His wife, Janice's mother, had left many years ago when Janice was only two years old. The last Ron Carson heard of his ex-wife was just about ten years ago, from a trucker friend that had seen her serving cocktails in one of the lesser hotels in the downtown area of Las Vegas.

Ron Carson knew his buddy wasn't telling him everything, but never pressed his friend for the real story, he just didn't care about her anymore and knew it wouldn't do any good to know the whole ugly truth. Sure his heart had hardened, but when you raise two girls on your own, you don't have much time to pine for a woman who left a note on your refrigerator.

Every week while Courtney and Janice were growing up, Ron Carson took his girls to the old chapel at the San Fernando Mission. It was a special and serene place, where he'd found his personal spiritual connection to God, and where he fervently hoped his young ladies would do the same.

The San Fernando Mission was the very cradle of the entire valley, holding its earliest recorded history deep inside its adobe walls. Ron Carson was drawn to the old gathering place where Fathers Serra and Crespi tamed a wilderness and guided native Californians on the path to Christianity. He developed a special kinship with these men that struggled long ago for the sake of goodness. He felt their presence in the old chapel, and it became an escape from his challenges and burdensome life.

It was not only the challenge of raising two young girls and piles of bills that weighed heavy, it was also the everyday toxic background noise that hummed in a monotonous frequency of decay—a decay that was apparent to him and any other person who gave a damn about the valley.

Even the ones that averted their eyes from the disease would never be immune to the large or small piece of chaos and heartache that was sure to come their way. But at the chapel, Ron Carson could shut out the cell phones, helicopters, graffiti, gunshots, threatening looks, gang symbols, poor school systems, and the perpetual silent apology for being a white middle-aged Catholic male.

Ron Carson's daughter Janice was the love of his life, but his life changed forever when he got the call from the police that day. About six months ago they called to tell him that she had died tragically alone in a motel room. It goes without saying that Ron was completed devastated and quite understandably hasn't recovered. Ron had given both his girls over to Hollywood unwillingly, and he cursed the day he took them both to meet with Fischer.

The tragedy was something her cousin Courtney had to avoid thinking about, for Janice was like a real sister to her. They had run off to Hollywood together, played together, flirted together and dabbled in the Lawrence Fischer high life together.

Until Janice's death, they both had semi-permanent suites at Fischer's estate in Bel Air. Like non-tenured employees, Lawrence Fischer always reminded the girls that they were replaceable, signifying the temporary status of their accommodations and all but implying the kind of payment he expected in return.

It turned out that Janice had a little more hunger for the drugs than Courtney did, and Lawrence Fischer was very happy to exploit that, exacting his payment in a twisted way. Quite typically with more and more drug use, Janice slowly changed, causing both girls to quarrel.

Not satisfied with merely using both young ladies for their bodies, Lawrence Fischer enjoyed seeing turmoil and strife between them, and took pride in ruining their sisterly relationship, purposely favoring one and shunning the other at certain key social events. Lawrence Fischer always preferred no alliance around him—not even a simple party of two. It was a security device of sorts—it was his way to avoid conspiracies.

With Janice's behavior becoming more and more erratic, and since Fischer could not be seen in public with anything but the finest arm candy, Courtney quickly became his exclusive showpiece.

Now, at the tender age of twenty, Janice realized she was already relegated to the status of a Hollywood has-been, and the promise of her Hollywood dream was revealed to be nothing more than a short-term sex contract. The young woman was angry, but she made her mind up that she wouldn't go down without a fight.

One evening, as Fischer prepared to take Courtney out, there was a violent confrontation, with vile words, and cutting accusations. Janice turned it up a notch by threatening to expose Lawrence Fischer to anyone that would listen.

"That will never happen my dear," Fischer warned.

Janice then packed a small bag, and stormed out of the estate checking into a seedy old motel on Ventura Boulevard. It was there that she launched her negative campaign, making call after call to anyone that would listen, warning all to beware of the evil bastard that was Lawrence Fischer.

The next afternoon she was found by a maid, hanging from a light fixture in the dingy motel room. The police investigated, and ruled it a simple suicide.

Even with their disagreements, Courtney loved her cousin more than anyone else on this earth; inherently knowing that Janice would never take her own life so easily or cheaply. Slowly, little by little, Courtney was waking up to the painful realization that Lawrence Fischer had to be involved in her death. She also knew that if she did not break away from this evil man soon, she would ultimately follow in her cousin's tragic footsteps.

She too had believed him when he promised the actress roles—first it was going to be just some television, then it would be an assured nomination for best supporting actress, so on, and so on. Her belief in him was solid and unshakable at first, but slowly, like ice melting in March, it got thinner and weaker with each passing day.

For a while she'd justified all of it, sure he was into kinky stuff, but she'd read about that kind of sex for years in the steamy articles of her women's magazines, the ones that sneaked past Ron Carson's better judgment. Sure, Fischer was abusive, but she had access to the limo, the place in Palm Springs, even an expense account at Barney's.

Now, she looked down at her bruises and knew that the unmentionable things she did with him and his vile friend Vince Shank, would most likely haunt her for the rest of her life. So, on this morning, after one of those nights, she made a promise to herself that something had to be done.

In truth, she had made this same promise to herself at least half a dozen times, but as always, when these mornings wore on, a cloudy denial would seep back into her thinking, helping her to rationalize that going to the commissary by herself, was a sufficiently rebellious and courageous act. Yes, this morning after was just like all the rest; the farthest she was going to run was across the lot for some green tea.

I'll show him. I won't come back for a least a whole hour, she thought.

Courtney didn't mix very well with many others on

the lot, deep down she always felt like an outsider with a constant elitist's disdain for the gypsy profession. The people around the studio that knew her were Fischer's drones and obviously couldn't be trusted. The ones that she didn't know saw her as just another struggling actress—a young girl that looked older than her years.

So, on her radical walk to the commissary, Courtney acted as usual, projecting the importance of being Fischer's girl by strutting her stuff—projecting her cool and sultry act out forty-foot in front of her, and letting her hippy, model runway walk bring up the rear.

Step by step, the old rationalization of her predicament was having an effect. She was lulling herself back into the sleep of the affluent, where knowing powerful people is a wonderful currency, more influential than gold, more intoxicating than cocaine, or exciting than sex.

Courtney again silently duped herself and fantasized about the fame that she knew would come—fame that was still within her grasp, still attainable, much more attainable from inside these studio walls than from outside them. Outside was now out of the question—outside was boring San Fernando, with a boring uncle, a boring chapel, and her boring life.

Courtney Carson performed her Best Supporting Actress role on this soundstage on February...

As she walked past a giant soundstage, her ego grabbed hold, and she could almost see her plaque hanging by the entrance. She then raised her nose up to her perceived station and enjoyed the knowing and sometimes lecherous looks from men and even women. She felt the warm intoxication of the illusion coming on, and like a fine cognac melting in her mouth, it made her bruises almost worth it.

Still, Courtney was a young lady at odds with herself. Yes, she hated her dull life, but after Janice had died, she hated the Hollywood life even more. As she walked to the commissary, her outsider's inner voice couldn't help critiquing nearly every person she saw.

There's Gustavo the cameraman, what a dull bore. He actually thinks that no one notices the cornrows of hair plugs on his bowling ball head. I so want to tell him to put a hat on, or just go and rip the plugs out. If you ever expect to get laid Gustavo, just own your baldness, you jackass.

Ugh, and here's Siobhan, the oh-so accomplished actress, yeah it's all about you Siobhan. That reminds me—I am so done with pretentious Celtic names.

It's a common behavior in this town, trash it and stomp it, but then resurrect it when you realize that you need it so very badly. She entered the commissary feeling conflicted, bought her tea, and chose a remote table far away from any positive-energy, yoga-powered actors.

As she sat sipping the green brew, an attractive man came over to her table. The vibes she sent out were either ignored or not picked up on because the jerk sat down anyway. She even threw him a quick "I'm annoyed" sideways glance in order to send the very clear message that it wasn't okay to violate her space—and this morning, her space took up just about one half of the entire commissary.

Usually, when throwing such a warning glance, she'd never attempt to make eye contact, as it was not the Hollywood way to be overly intimate when you had an unpleasant agenda to attend to. Like flipping the middle finger from the comfort of your luxury car, it wasn't necessary to exchange any real communication as personal as a direct glance.

However, this time, something led her to look straight up his body, from his handsome suit, up to his gorgeous face, then deep into his fantastic brown eyes. They were magnificent eyes, with a depth of beauty and presence like none she had ever seen in her life, certainly they were nothing at all like the dead malignant eyes of Lawrence Fischer. This man looked like the kind of man that you could ask important questions of, for his presence held a weight—one part valor, and one part charity.

"Hello," he said.

"What?" she replied in short, bitchy fashion.

Not scaring easily, he kept his smile and softly repeated his introduction.

"Hello."

She had all to do but laugh.

Who is this dweeb? she thought to herself. *He isn't important if I don't know him."*

"How are you?" he persisted, though again she ignored him.

"I'm truly sorry to bother you. I just started working on the lot, and I really don't know anyone," he told her.

She angrily adjusted in her chair and after breathing a disgruntled breath said:

"Okay, Mister noob, here's commissary rule number one; when someone is quietly sipping their tea—let them sit *quietly* and sip their tea."

Although her delivery was stern, it was stern in a Shirley MacLaine sort of way. Shirley always had a smile behind every line she'd ever spoken. He glanced at her again and smiled, although he couldn't help but notice the bruises on her wrists and arms. Then he held out his hand for hers.

"My name's Dennis... what's yours?"

CHAPTER 13

THE MYSTERY OF THE MATTRESSES

THE DELUSION OF denial, when it comes to failure is quite insidious. On one hand, you don't ever want to have your present dim view of the world prevent any possible future successes, for the best way to ensure things will go badly is to remain inside the stinking thinking of a person who is hard done by. On the other hand, when bad luck seems to hound you for years, denial may be the only way to deal with the possibility that a dark force may be wreaking havoc in your life. Until my recent events, I never thought it possible.

Throughout time, there have been cultures that believed fervently in curses and hexes, and in those societies, ostracism and/or banishment of the inflicted were quite common. Even today in Southern California, those who lack fortune will surely suffer a sharp drop in their social and business calendars.

In more primitive cultures, specialists who were

concerned enough with the afflicted's problem, attempted to cure them of their ills for the greater betterment of their respective societies. The methods were voodoo, exorcism, flogging and sometimes, burning at the stake.

Here in Hollywood, we treat our afflicted with our very own scarlet letters. Conveniently, the letters always spell out the loser's name, issuing a warning to all to beware of the unlucky bastard. Our witch doctors are those that broadcast infomercials selling positive-thinking and self-empowered solutions to drunks and insomniacs at four a.m.

Today is August 1. The curtain has opened on summer's last act, and I sit in the audience alone. This is the month when so many of my friends go away on all-expense – paid vacations to Palm Springs, Hawaii, Big Bear or Monterey. Quite usually, they're guests of their friends in higher places. When you are on the A-list, you get those and other perks, but when you drop down off that list, you get to pet-sit the pooches and kitties of the A-listers. That's the way it rolls in sunny old So-Cal.

I promised I would be a good pal and take care of Natasha, my friend Sandra's German shepherd, while Sandra and her fiancé are away in Maui. Natasha is a fierce, but aging dog that took me months to get used to. Of course, that depends on which end of the telescope you're on.

Surely, Natasha's take is that it took her months in order for her to not want to rip my face off. However, once we became pals, we developed a wonderful man/ dog relationship, and she now warmly welcomes me, as opposed to barking or snarling as she used to. Upon greeting her, I pick her up like a big four legged baby, give her a kiss on the head, and tell her that I love her.

As Natasha and I walk down Ventura Boulevard on her out-and-about, I hear a whirring sound. Sure enough, a mattress truck pulls over to the curb just a few feet in front of us. Natasha, who usually wants to eat all strangers, lies down and wags her tail as the very large driver gets out of the truck.

Yes it's him again, Roberto—the man who saved me.

Natasha remains silent and calm as he approaches, which is a first for this dog. Usually any stranger that even dares to get close to me is severely warned by her vicious sounding deep bark and exposed gnashing teeth. He smiles at Natasha, then adjusts his shirt and straightens his straw hat, obviously taking pride in his massive appearance.

"Hello again, Tru-man... you have the questions?"

Roberto pronounces my name "True Man" and looks even larger than he did down by the river.

Without the blinding fear I had for him in our previous meeting, I now notice that he bears the remnants of what looks to be an old gang tattoo on his arm. He also looks like the kind of man that could pick you up with one hand then flick you across the four-lane boulevard with a simple snap of his wrist. To be quite honest, I am happy to see the man who saved my life.

"Questions? You could say that, Roberto. Here's one; why does this man-eater of a dog lie down and smile at you, and what's with these trucks and the mattresses? Excuse me if I sound annoyed, but I've met face to face with two very evil people."

"They are devils, amigo—do not be in denial," Roberto interrupts.

His firm gaze injects a near-nauseating, hyper-reality into the moment. I stare in stunned silence for a short moment, while my tone finds a lower, more serious timbre.

"Okay, then why don't they just kill me and get it over with? I haven't been as much as spit at, well that bastard Vince floated up to me and nearly caused me to crap my pants, but besides that and some brain teasers from Fischer—nothing."

Roberto listens to my rant and doesn't pay me much mind, averting his eyes and pursing his large mouth. It's almost as if he's heard these complaints and questions hundreds of times.

"Our trucks are the antennas, amigo, " Roberto answers.

"Your mattress trucks are antennas?"

Roberto looks at me in reverent silence as if he is thinking of someone or something that requires more than ordinary seriousness.

"Yes, Tru-man, antennas. We get messages, send messages, and, you know; stay in touch."

"Messages from where?" I ask apprehensively. Then add, "Hey—if they're devils—who are you?"

"Us? Well, I guess we didn't tell you—we are los angeles, and we weren't named after the city, it's the city that was named after us."

Roberto then smiles a giant's smile.

I didn't know whether to laugh, cry, or strip off my clothes and run into the road.

"You're angels... with pickup trucks and antenna mattresses."

"Well, put it this way, we monitor the bad, Tru-man. We patrol the valley and help rid *el diablos*. You were chosen because we have seen what's in your heart. You're so done with these devils, and you could never work for them again, even if you wanted to. You're gifted, Tru-man, protected too, but listen to me good— you can still fail and be defeated.

"Like Asher Corrigan, if they want to be released, they need to ask you to release them. If they don't want to be released, they need to be vanquished. We've shown you an easy, and a hard one, so now it's time for you to step up and realize that you have a new job. We know you're not perfect, Tru-man, you're a wavy line for sure, but the road to righteousness is drawn with many wavy lines."

I looked at Roberto and couldn't help returning a

nervous smile, a smile that he didn't appreciate, for his tone darkened.

"Hey, amigo... this is serious business. I know Asher told you a little about what had to be done—we knew you wouldn't do it because you weren't ready, but now you're ready. Tru-man, If they won't be released, you must kill them, and believe me if you do, you are doing them and all of your people a favor."

Roberto paused, smiled a bit, then continued:

"You're growing into a warrior, but remember there's a fine line. Too much hatred is darkness. A desire for eliminating evil is different, it's not hate, for us it is a necessary goodness. Look to your heart... you'll always know the difference."

He takes another pause in his instruction. He knows that I'm frightened. Putting his massive hand on my shoulder, he softens his tone a notch.

"This can be very dangerous, and you must remember this important rule; once you try to kill them, your protection is over, and they can come at you—and make no mistake, they sure as hell will."

My smile disappears and is replaced by an involuntary fear-induced downturn of my eyes and mouth. The gravity of his words makes me not want to look at Roberto, but a glance at Natasha reveals that she's completely enraptured by him.

"Tru-man, listen to me, you are ready now—you must kill them, quick and true. To kill them you need to have emotional attachment with them. You cannot just go at them—it won't work."

As he says "emotional attachment," he uses his hands to punctuate the syllables as if he were taught to pronounce his second language words that way. Looking at him, I see that Roberto has a human side and although he obviously possesses extraordinary powers, his humanity shows in small things, such as perspiration and an occasional cough or rub of his eye.

"So what happens, Roberto, if I can't kill the head of the biggest movie studio in town, and if I do, how the hell will I get away with it?"

"If you can't kill him, someone will, but then you'll be..."

I didn't need for him to complete the sentence.

"On the other hand when you are successful, you will have no worries about the law, we have already taken care of all that human stuff."

"Okay sure, Roberto, this totally sounds like a piece of cake."

When there's a language barrier, one of the first casualties of communication is the misunderstanding of slang—and sarcastic slang only makes matters worse. I don't know if Roberto understands the "piece of cake" phrase, but never the less, I get his cold answer in reply.

"Six devils, Tru-man, six devils must go."

Again, a loud homing device sound emits from inside the truck. The man scans the horizon as his eyes glaze over.

"We've been calling to you for years, Truman."

"What do you mean calling to me?"

"Some will be easy—"

I interrupt, "Yeah, I know—some will be hard."

Natasha barks as he turns preparing to leave, then she begins to pull me back to her home.

"You too girl!" Roberto calls to Natasha. "Hey, Truman, nice dog. She's a good girl, she'll be something on the other side this dog—big guardian, and she can't wait."

Then the giant man takes out a pad and pencil from his shirt pocket.

"What's your cell number in case I have to call you?" he adds.

I give him my number with the area code being 8-1-8.

"Ahaaa, the 8-1-8 code. I figured you for a 2-1-3 dude. It's not a mistake this 8-1-8 area code for the valley. You do see that it's the split infinity, yes?"

I guess the look on my face betrays my confusion because Roberto begins to laugh.

"Alright, one step at a time, Tru-man. Little baby steps today… okay?"

Then, he gets back into his truck, waves, and shouts like a Mexican Santa Claus:

"*Adios*, amigos!"

Natasha barks at him and has never looked more pleased.

I know now that Lawrence Fischer wants me angry.

He thinks I'll react wildly and then become an easy target for his counterattack. I'm not that stupid. He showed me those horrific images of Sherry in order to get me to lash out, and it very nearly worked.

I drive east down Ventura Boulevard running from the late afternoon sun towards my place. I pass through Studio City crossing Laurel Canyon, and think about making a right so I could head up into the hills to find what's left of Joni Mitchell, Jackson Browne, and the ghosts of the Laurel Canyon scene. Instead, I drive past and stop into Du-Par's for a slice of blueberry pie.

I sit at the counter and enjoy my pie. I also realize that I am coming to the end of my time here in the valley. I don't know where I will move on to, but I can see the end in the waitress's face when she brings me my check.

I continue on my way past the studio lot. The water tower stares down at me and silently issues a warning. I lower my gaze and once again see that Midwest-looking father at the studio gate—the man who wants to see Lawrence Fischer.

I pull over and watch his heated exchange with the security officers for the second time. This encounter ends with the same result as the first, for the man is turned around and angrily drives away from the lot. Something tells me this man can be useful, so I decide to follow him.

CHAPTER 14

DAUGHTER JANICE

WE WIND OUR way over to the Hollywood Freeway, taking it north, then after a short while, merge onto the Interstate 5. I glance down at my gas gauge just in case the man I'm following is driving way upstate. As it turns out, he gets off at the top of the valley in the namesake town of San Fernando. I follow, though not too closely, making a left onto San Fernando Mission Boulevard, approaching the mission itself.

The San Fernando Mission, like all of California's other missions, serves as a living monument to some of the states earliest recorded history. It also holds some of California's more recent history, and being a record junkie, I can't help but think of Buddy Holly's death mate, Ritchie "La Bamba" Valens, who happens to be buried there. From the outside front, it looks quite beautiful, and I make a mental note to bring Jane up here for a visit.

This dad guy hasn't noticed that I've been following

him until now, for he just slammed on his brakes and pulled over, directly in front of the mission. My first inclination is to keep on driving by, but quickly reconsider, realizing that I need to speak with this man and might as well do it right here.

I pull up directly behind him, and at once he gets out of his car and walks back towards mine rather slowly. As I roll down my crank window, I find myself staring at another loaded gun. This one is almost jokingly wrapped in a paper bag with the end ripped out so as to avoid detection.

"Take it easy bro," I tell him.

"Don't call me bro, dickwad. Are you one of Fischer's boys?" he asks. "This ain't much of a hot rod if you are."

Now, being that my bone-stock 1964 Dodge is even being associated with what I consider a lesser hot rod, I am moved to pipe up.

"Listen, take it slow okay—I'm not with Fischer. If you want Fischer, then we have a lot in common. I just noticed that you were trying to get onto the lot—I thought we should talk."

On the mantle, over the long since unusable, earthquake-disabled fireplace, rest several pictures of his daughter at various ages, from infancy, to pre-teen, to adulthood. The most unfortunate picture in the group is one of the Virgin Mary on a funeral mass card.

When children bury their parents it is always sad, but it's the natural order of things. When parents bury their children, it's a damned tragedy, and just not the way it's supposed to go. I also notice another photo of a different young lady, one that bears a remarkable resemblance to the leather-panted hot rod girl that carjacked me on the lot.

"The name's Morrow, Truman Morrow, and I happen to be in a similar situation. I really can't say too much more, but as I told you, I want to get to Fischer myself."

"Why?" he asks pointedly.

"Let's just say that I want him to go away and stop ruining so many people's lives."

"I'm Ron Carson. Let me ask you this, Truman. What's your end in all of this—who'd he hurt in your world?"

He seemed to be challenging me to meet or surpass the level of his burden. Knowing that I'm not in the same emotional league as him I flippantly respond:

"Ron, I guess you could say that I am just trying to get out of LA."

Ron smiles slightly and nods his head up and down. It seems to be in agreement with what I'd said, and even a possible acceptance of me as a comrade.

"She was a great kid. She was my whole world."

I can't help but notice that his whole world is now an unkempt dark, silent and dusty home sweltering in the valley. This poor man appears to be done with life, he looks tired, crushed and robbed. It makes me sad,

maybe because part of me could identify with his help-
lessness and anger.

"And who's that other young lady?" I ask, pointing
to the photo of the teen.

"Well, that's my daughter too, her name is
Courtney. She's my niece by birth, my brother's kid
that I adopted. For a while, I blamed her because she
was always so gung-ho on becoming a star, even when
she was small... but they both ran off together, nobody
twisted Janice's arm."

Yes, I'm sure of it now. That's her, the one that carjacked me.

After a long pause, Ron Carson wipes a tear away
in manly fashion, sniffing and pretending to clear his
throat, then, continues his sad saga.

"They were introduced to Lawrence Fischer by
this older lady that used to manage my ex-wife,
Janice's mother, then everything moved real fast. One
of Fischer's men got Janice and Courtney a few audi-
tions, he even took them out on the town a few times.
First I was on board with it, but then they started staying out all night. Then, after their big meeting on the
lot with Fischer, they just never came home. I haven't
heard a peep from Courtney—she came to the funeral,
but didn't even say a single word. She was whisked off
in a limo right after it was over. He had his punk goons
all around her."

"Your ex-wife was in show business?" I ask gently.

"If you could call it that. Yeah, an actress, actually

she was more of a professional auditioner—she didn't work much, except for that one early film."

"And who was this lady that used to manage your wife?"

"Her name was Mae, my ex signed with her about twenty years ago—did that one decent film, then we kind of got together."

I try not to telegraph my dark surprise. Remaining motionless, an ice chill forms like a storm over my head. It's the jagged blue light again, which I now guess is a rush of whatever enzyme your brain uses to suppress fear and shock. To steady myself, I sit down in order to ask my next question.

"This lady, Mae," I softly clear my throat. "Was her last name McLaughlin?"

With a dramatic pause, Ron Carson thinks, then, releases his answer.

"Yeah, I think so. You knew her? Small world."

It felt as if supernovas were about to collide over the small worlds of these affairs. I try to remain calm and keep my expression as blank as possible with my reply.

"Yes, I knew her for a long time. In fact, I first met her many years ago, just about the time when your ex-wife would have been managed by her."

Ron looks at me with suspicion for about a second, then obviously dismisses whatever he was thinking, opens a drawer and pulls out an eight by ten of his wife, which he hands to me.

"Does this face ring a bell?"

Ringing is not exactly the word I would have used, it's more like a painful clanging, made worse by having to clench my jaw in suppression of a deep, sad moan.

There she is, Erica—my Erica, that gorgeous young woman that bore the sun in her eyes and the sky in her smile. The one that made me trek west, and caused Sherry to follow. The one that could sell the California lie to the hardest of Easterners. The one I made passionate love to every night for my entire stay. The one that Mae introduced me to, and upon returning to New York, the one I heard was with child. Mae's voice rings clearly in my ears:

She just up and left the business—she met some guy and got into trouble.

Keeping my outward composure, I tell a lie to Ron Carson.

"Sorry, her face doesn't ring a bell. I've never seen her before."

Ron appears to believe it.

"She was wild, Truman, but I loved her. I met her when I was working as a grip, early in my career. We went to a party, had a few drinks and ended up driving to Tijuana for the weekend. You know, crazy youth stuff. Then, a week or so later she showed up on my doorstep with a single bag and a very bad black eye. She told me a nasty producer gave it to her, some guy named Shank—I looked for the bastard, but he hid pretty well."

Ron looks down and takes a breath, then continues the sad tale.

"She told me that she was done with the movie business and wanted stability, so we were married the following week... right over here at the old chapel. Erica's eye never really healed that well, so we didn't take many wedding pictures, and I think that's really the reason she stopped acting. Around eight months later, Janice came along—just a bit premature. She was fine though, no troubles with my baby girl."

I walk back over to the mantle with all the pictures of the young Janice. I don't know if I'm imagining it, but I see hints of my grandmother, my father, even my sister in her face. There's no way to know for sure—but I could swear that I'm looking at my daughter.

The age makes perfect sense, she was just about nine months older than the last time I saw Erica. I feel it deeply, so deeply that it burns with pain. My heart cries out in silence for her and her mother.

I suppress the urge to be sick right here on the floor, and ask Ron if he has any booze. I pretend to want to raise a toast to our new understanding. Usually, I'd only drink Mr. Daniel's fine spirit, but at this moment, I'd drink any rotgut the dusty town of San Fernando could offer up in order to numb the sharp, disturbing pain that is stabbing at my stomach and heart.

"Hell, I could use one too. I think I have some Jack Daniel's in the kitchen cabinet."

I consider this stroke of coincidental luck the first

concrete sign of a higher power working in my favor throughout this entire affair, and so I down a hefty gulp—then a few more, all the time acting as if my heart isn't ripping into Shakespearean shreds.

Each time Ron leaves the room, I take Erica's eight by ten and steal a look, then walk over to the mantle and wonder as deep as any man has wondered since the dawn of creation.

"He killed her. He killed her as sure as you are sitting on that couch, Truman. He promised her the world, told her to lose weight, did God knows what to her, introduced her around to all the rest of the Hollywood scum, and then just cut her off. How is he going to pay for that? What about my niece? She still lives with him and is also doing God knows what with him."

Ron Carson pulls out a DVD and pushes it into the player straining to see the "play" button.

"Truman, my baby could dance, sing... she was wonderful."

I don't want to watch it, and think about coming up with an excuse to find the door, but the afternoon is so filled with pathos already that I just let it wash over me.

What I watch brings me to tears—a little girl dancing, singing, loving the praise her mom and dad heap on her. Truly heartbreaking when you know where it all leads. The images stoke my painful allegory—a woman I loved, and most likely, my child, a child that I never got to hold.

"Dancing lessons, singing lessons, diction classes.

I was her cheerleader. Now I wish I would have punished her."

"It probably wouldn't have done any good to do that, she most likely would have wanted it more," I tell him.

"I suppose you're right. When she died, the police said it was suicide, but I know it wasn't. He did it, Truman."

The booze had begun to show its affects in Ron's behavior, and he paused a moment before continuing with some very serious words.

"He's evil, plain evil, and guess what? I'm going to fucking kill him."

His desperate words rang out, leaving a tense silence in their wake.

"You won't be able to," I whisper. My words are covered and obscured by the still-present ambience of his serious statement. So I try again, this time raising my voice a little louder.

"You won't be able to get to him... not him. He hides behind the studio walls. He knows who you are, and so does security. Ron—you'll never get in."

If I weren't in the middle of a supernatural event, I would definitely tell this man that it isn't worth it—to just go on and live his life. However, knowing his whole life was his daughter, I let him have his hate—because it just may be the only thing that he's got left.

As it turns out, the sad revelations were not finished for the day, and he tells me more about Erica.

"Her mother disappeared years back. She would come in and out, and go back and forth to Vegas, then one day—she just stayed there. About a month before my baby girl passed, I heard her mother Erica was found dead in a motel room in Sparks, Nevada. She was clutching a photo of our baby Janice and quite strangely, some necklace with a little Christmas tree on it."

The whiskey couldn't help me anymore. My heart broke in half. The layers of pain and tragedy forced tears from my eyes, and thankfully Ron Carson was facing away towards the mantle allowing me to the opportunity to hide, and to wet my sleeves.

With the tearing of my heart, I realized that real truths never change—even beyond death. Supposed truths that do change reveal themselves to be merely fads or passing feelings. The truths that hurt like hell when they bend or break are the real McCoy, and like them or not, they are the fiber of human life.

At this very moment, I took another step away from Hollywood, and knew that I'd better get busy and find someone—someone to start a family with, someone to help me place pictures on my mantle. My pictures will stay, and God willing, my kids will bear the correctly ordered burden of burying me first.

CHAPTER 15

BEWITCHED

MOST PEOPLE AREN'T very introspective or self-analyzing even in the happiest of times, and when they are stressed with failure, loss or heartache, it becomes damned near impossible to be impartial and assess your own mental state. After finding out about Erica, and then of course with the strong possibility that Janice was my daughter, I have fallen to a place where I can't seem to keep my hands on my own controls.

I think about seeing a shrink, but then reject it out of hand almost immediately. What would I tell him?

"Hey, Doc, I have this problem—there's this devil that's the head of the studio, and these guys that carry mattresses are the angels."

I don't think that I'd get too many more sentences out before the funny wagon dragged me away for about two or three years. This is a lonely problem. What I'm going through is obviously so far out of the ordinary that it would be wrong to expect any ordinary person to understand it.

What scares me is the knowledge that paranoid schizophrenia can be just as realistic to the sufferer as this is to me, so I decide to take the interim step and go see my regular physician and feel him out on the symptoms of mental disease.

On the way over to the doctor's office, I look in my rear view mirror and see two mattress trucks about four or five car lengths back behind me on Ventura Boulevard. Pulling into the doctor's parking lot, my phone sounds the alert noting that I've received a text. I continue to patrol the lot looking for a space and check my cell... sure enough there is a text from Roberto and another from Armando.

From Armando: *Crazy peoples shouldn't text and drive.*

And from Roberto: *Save the co-pay, buy us a coffee.*

There isn't a psychiatrist in the world that could have been as effective as these guys are with their sarcastic diagnosis of reality, and certainly none that could make me laugh as much.

I decide to blow off the doctor and take both Roberto and Armando over to Jerry's Deli where we sit at the counter. I guess angels don't carry any money because instead of coffee, they both con me into a bowl of Jerry's fantastic matzo ball soup with the bagel chips on the side. These boys sure know their San Fernando Valley food.

The conversation is light, and we don't discuss the

devils at all, we just talk like friends—well, with a slight language barrier at times. I found out that Roberto is a Dodgers fan and Armando is quite appropriately an Angels fan. They rib each other about the differences in the National and American leagues, and all at once I feel warm and comfortable. I proceed to tell them that it's a known fact that the New York Yankees are the greatest team that baseball has ever seen—to which they both respond in unison:

"We *hate* the Yankees."

Which of course brings my knee jerk, automatic, snide retort:

"Get in line."

We all laughed deep and hard. The check is more than the doctor's co-pay would have been, but I enjoyed every second I've spent with them—I really like these guys. I don't know if they put some kind of voodoo on my head, but I never once thought of asking them a single worried question, my supernatural trouble never even crossed my mind.

After we part, I begin my drive home happy for two reasons; first, I'm sure now that I'm really experiencing what I'm going through, and second, tonight's the big night—Jane's cooking me dinner at her apartment.

Driving back, I think back to when I was a small boy, back when I felt such incredible wonder at the simplest things—my laughter, pure and simple over plain delights such as a crisp summer day—just my bicycle and I sitting alone in an empty school field, looking over at my former classroom now silent and empty, feeling the grass tips with the palm of my hands, then deciding when and where I'd go next, independent for the first time in my young life. My feelings for Jane are akin to those times, those simplicities, with all the delight, wonder and pure human truth.

When a man is first interested in a woman, he sizes up her charm and behaviors to those of his male buddies. It's true, we choose our male buddies and new female acquaintances for the joy they offer.

When romance ensues and things get more serious, that's when fun starts to take a back seat and a more critical assessment of the pairing takes over. Usually, that's when the trouble starts—who bought this, who should pay for that, who cleans this, who fixes that? An old friend used to call it "going for territory."

Jane and I are new, and it's truly fun to be with her, but I can feel my heart starting to look for the long lasting binds that could carry us on to the harder parts. So for now, I file away any question I have about Jane and her possible involvement with these supernatural events.

Standing at her door, I press her buzzer hiding the simple bouquet behind my back. She comes to the door and looks more than stunning in her neat and understated way, then welcomes me with a soft kiss from her gorgeous lips.

There are candles burning an indescribable scent, luring me into her small living room. She puts on the classic *Sinatra/Chobim* bossa nova album, and immediately, I am lost in her charms.

You know the feeling, when you are so impressed by someone that you want everything that they have in their home, and want to live just as they do. Candles, glasses, a great rug, food, even special wooden clothes hangers—everything looks so good and right to me. This will be one of those nights when I go back home and straighten up my place in order to feel better about it and myself.

She brings me a cocktail, and hands it to me from behind as I sit on her enveloping couch. I love the touch of her hand steadying mine as I reach back for the drink. She knew enough not to put a lime in my Jack and Coke, but I am not surprised as she is quickly becoming my dream woman.

A wonderful dinner is simmering on her stove—a little white stove, as clean as a whistle, one that fits perfectly in her tidy place. If this is her way of going for territory, she can take as much of it as she likes.

All of a sudden, just tonight, right here, for the first time since leaving New York, I crave books. I want to read again—leave the valley sunshine behind, close the drapes, open one up and visit a faraway place with a great detective, or even with another lonely man searching for a soul he could run towards.

I haven't read as much as a magazine article in many months, so it thrills me just to look at her impressive bookcase. It looks like she has a few early Fitzgerald books with their bluish Scribner's binding and faded golden titles on the spine, as well as some poetry, history, and mystery titles. It's a small but impressive collection.

I hear the plop of the record changer dropping another platter down, and wait with anticipation through the initial scratchy pops of the lead-in groove. Ella Fitzgerald is telling us about her crush on another, in her sultry version of "Bewitched, Bothered and Bewildered." I can identify.

A pop of a wine cork, and I am indeed delighted with the direction that the evening is taking. A little wine buzz on top of my Jack Daniel's will ease the unwelcome supernatural angst that is hovering in the back of my mind. The chardonnay melts like oak soaked butter over my tongue, upping the warmth of my pleasure and enjoyment.

I'm having one of *those* moments, the ones Fitzgerald spoke about in his short story "Winter Dreams." The ones you take with you to your grave, and by the grace of God, will revisit, forever young in paradise. This shining moment, usually reserved for youth, has visited upon and chosen me to delight and shine in it. How lucky am I, Ella? Sing for me.

Dinner:
Broiled Bay Scallops in white wine, over Risotto
Broccoli Rabe, sautéed in garlic and oil
Vintage California Chardonnay
Dessert:

Italian Cheesecake

Espresso with a lemon peel twist

After Dinner Entertainment:

Poetry Readings (From memory only)

Passages from Fitzgerald's *The Love of The Last Tycoon*

With the winding down of the evening's festivities, we bond in a special way. No mindless TV watching, no talk of business or of the lack of business. No hatred for mankind or politics. Just us immersed in warmth, great food, slight touches, and some long simmering looks between us.

At this moment, my life feels complete. I am happy and whole. I feel comfortable in my own skin. I haven't been able to feel this for years and years—always wanting something else, always needing more, and never feeling that I'd gotten it. Always wishing I was somewhere else or somewhere better while lost days and years ticked off the calendar. Here, with her, I can talk freely, I can breathe deep and easy. Right here, right now I am a happy man.

I tried not to think too much about Janice and Erica as I plunge into this moment. I'm seeking shelter here tonight, and though it may speak volumes about my fractured state, it's no matter, for right now it's all okay— right now is enough.

I nearly announce out loud that this evening could not move any higher or get any better. I'm satisfied with it just the way it is. In my younger day the main course and purpose of my visit, even if I were respectfully smitten, would be the physical conclusion and sexual fulfillment of the evening.

Strange, as I gaze into her eyes, seeing the flickering candle reflected from the corner, I realize that I could stop right here and be quite satisfied. (Maybe this is what women always go on about?) Touching her hand slowly, teasingly and timidly, reaching for it across the couch, finding her fingers then intertwining with them ever so slowly, is as sensual and thrilling as any human experience I've ever had.

However, I am a man. The man-chemicals take over, and my finger reaching advances to other places, then slowly, I begin to realize that I was quite wrong about the perceived apex of the evening.

CHAPTER 16

CAROLINE, NO

"LET YOURSELF IN," Vince Shank calls to the beautiful lady as she opens the door to his condo unit. Vince steps into the shower and a singsong slur of words drifts out in a most lecherous tone:

"It's on the table, baby girl."

Sherry looks for her prize as a predator would, scanning the two tabletops within sight. First, the dining table, with its dusty magazines and junk mail, then the coffee table, dirty, stained and chipped. There, her eyes find what she had come for; the pink package neatly folded like a tiny envelope containing the powdery hell that screamed out to her, telling her the most exhilarating and wonderful lies, the kind that made her breath a little more shallow and caused her heart to race.

She was beyond tears at this point, she would save those for when she was coming down, but right now, she needed to numb her brain and body in preparation for the onslaught that would soon be visited upon her by Mr. Vince Shank. The price to pay was dear, the man was rough, and her bruises and welts, though well hidden, told the clear story; this was addiction.

Vince Shank was a nasty man. He was pure evil, as evil as Lawrence Fischer. The main difference between them was Fischer's vast intellect in comparison with Shank's common limitations.

His lack of smarts got him booted off Fischer's lot a few years back, kicked out to Santa Monica and his runner-up video game gig. Dumb people make stupid decisions, and even today he was foolish enough to trust Sherry and take his sweet time in the shower.

The thought of what Shank was about to do to her body wasn't enough to stop her from snorting, slurping, and licking the last grain of the powder from the mirror, but it was enough to affect her after the drug was consumed.

There's a funny thing about most addicts; their high is actually their natural state, so when they're not loaded they're completely out of sorts. There's that scant moment or two after they get high when they're levelheaded and clear thinking and usually this occurs in the minutes right before the debilitating effects of the drug carry off all sense and physical coordination. In this clear moment, Sherry rises and shakes, but thinks deep with conscious thought—the kind that she uses when she writes in her diary.

She sees herself in the dirty mirror over the couch and is ashamed of what she's become. She's worn thin;

the spark that attracted so many young men has dulled like old silver.

In her back pocket is an envelope folded over with several old photographs inside. She taps it through her jeans to be sure it hasn't dislodged, which also serves as a reminder of its pending, important delivery. She'll make sure it's secure in her pocket several times before the rapidly moving blood carrying the dissolved powder reaches her brain bringing on its numb, inebriated state.

With one last long look in the mirror, the remainder of the good woman inside the junkie's body seizes the initiative and bolts from the filthy room, out into the burning valley sun. She trots past the pool, and across the courtyard, passing some gossipy neighbors staring in her direction. Casting aside shame, Sherry patters down the terra cotta steps into the echoing, hard-surfaced, plastic-plant lobby, then goes out the double doors, leaving her echo behind.

The effects of the drug begin to grab hold of her legs, arms and eyes as she gets near to the boundary of the complex, then staggering slightly, she bears down with clenched teeth in the struggle to remain in focus and control.

She doesn't hear the running footsteps until they are nearly upon her—footsteps from the demon Shank, in boxer shorts, still dripping from the shower, his fist clenched and raised in anticipation of violently giving another dumb broad a well deserved black eye.

Her dad must have sensed Sherry's peril on one of her trips back East, for a loving father will do anything to insure his daughter's safety, and his gift for her turned out to be a very well placed gesture of his affection.

His disgusting groans are what give Vince away, prompting Sherry to calmly wheel around and raise her father's thoughtful present. It was common for her to carry the small pistol out on her dark adventures of late, but this is the first time that it's drawn out of her purse in self-defense.

Her timing is wise, and her blunt aim true, as the two shots punch violently out of the gun. The spent .380 shells spin around in the air, hit the puddle at the curb and hiss slightly while the victim falling into the same, sloshes his hands through the muck, fruitlessly crawling towards his executioner.

The groan of the man-devil is obviously heard for blocks around, for the many dogs in the neighborhood howl in unison for nearly a full ten seconds.

*

Hearing the dogs, I jolt awake from my afternoon nap. Leaping to my feet I pray that my visions weren't real, but know instinctively and without question that there is something very, very wrong.

The steel gate bangs wildly off the brick building as I bash through the side exit, then rings back into its catch as I run out towards the street. At the same moment, the letter from the Mattress Men buzzes in my pocket as if pleading a warning.

Coming upon my dear sweet friend, I find her standing calmly, looking more beautiful than ever—her chest heaving with heavy breath, and her eyes fighting through drugs as they slowly turn to meet mine.

We hardly notice the police streaming down the block, or the stares from the gathering horrified crowds. Our loving gaze is interrupted only briefly when Sherry hands me the important envelope from her pocket.

On the outside it's marked:

Photos — Do not open until NY.

I don't understand what it means, but don't question it either.

A young police officer runs over and tackles Sherry down onto the grass at the curb. The gun falls from her hand as silent as its victim, Vince Shank, now and forever prevented from hurting the young or the weak— Vince Shank, dead.

Sherry is led to the police car with her hands cuffed behind her back.

"Release me!" she screams, not to the police officer guiding her, but to someone behind me.

To my surprise, I turn around to see four Mattress Men including a very tough looking Roberto, and he smiles at me with only his serene, nearly luminescent eyes. Then turning his gaze towards Sherry, Roberto raises a soft finger and points to me, and in that moment Sherry and I both realize who we really are.

Sherry smiles and laughs happily through tears.

"Oh thank God," she cries, and nearly collapses until she's steadied by the police officer.

Overcoming my breaking heart, I calmly, but resolutely answer:

"You are released."

My voice sounds as if it came out of someone else—it was the voice of a serious person, a person of conviction. Hooray and surprise for the man who is persona non grata.

Sherry lights up and smiles the most loving smile for me, pure love in its essential form, and as odd as it sounds as she was about to be locked up, she never looked freer.

An amazing change comes over her, and I see the Sherry I once knew. The junkie is now gone, and a light shines from her face, a light that would have been cherished by a great cinematographer had she ever had the chance to fulfill her dreams.

There are precious moments of change that come naturally in life, like moving from a home, or graduating from a school. In these moments, when it's time to say goodbye, it never feels real, though deep down you know; this is the last time, this is the end. Sadly, our broken relationship only briefly sustains this loving apex, for within seconds it's quickly ended by the aggressive young policeman.

I glance down at the Six Devils letter and notice that indeed she is number four. It all makes sense in my small world, but not in my large. My large world cannot bear the scope of all this.

"Easy on her!" a young, well-dressed LAPD detective shouts to the adrenaline-excited uniformed officer pushing her into the car.

I could swear the detective gave Roberto a knowing glance, with Roberto nodding quietly in return. The detective takes over for the younger officer and softly guides Sherry into the back of the car. He gets in with her and closes the door, and they drive off west, melting into the valley's oppressive sun.

About three hours later my cell phone rings. It's the man that took Sherry in, Detective Vega, and his tone is stern. What I thought would be a thorough questioning of me to be used in evidence against Sherry, turns out to be much worse indeed.

"Mr. Morrow, we tried to find some of her family here, but could find no one, so I thought that I should call and tell you."

I'm afraid of what he has to tell me because detectives don't usually deliver good news.

"I am very sorry to inform you that Sherry went into cardiac arrest on the way to the station—she died on the way to the hospital."

My mind goes numb and my heart nearly stops. I knew I was involved in a serious game, but I had no idea that this would be one of the results.

"I don't want you to blame yourself, you did all that you could do to save her," he tells me.

"I didn't save her——I can't save anyone."

I said it, and I meant it. I knew I was not here to save, but to release or slay, and if releasing someone has this effect, well then it's the same damned thing.

"She was headed for doom with Shank," Detective Vega advises. "We knew he was a drug dealer—it was inevitable."

He said some more comforting words to me, but I didn't pay much attention. When he hung up, I was slightly surprised that he didn't have any official questions for me. Cops always have paperwork, and they fill up that paperwork by asking questions. Detective Vega didn't ask me a single one.

*

I hid in my condo for about three days, avoiding talking to the press, the neighbors, and even Jane. I was physically sick for about two of those days, and on the third day, pulled myself up and took stock of my responsibilities.

What I've become is not something that I ever intended to become, but with the death of Sherry I knew my job was a serious one, and the likes of Lawrence Fischer needed to go the way of Vince Shank. I wasn't scared one damned bit at this point. Now, all at once, I accepted it——I was a hard-assed warrior.

The week after Sherry left us was filled with responsibility owed to her, and since I was the only friend she had left, it all fell to me. I was the welcoming party for her distraught family who came from back East to bury her. I thought it strange that they wanted her laid to rest out here in the valley, but her mother explained their family's feelings.

"Sherry wasn't herself when she'd visit us back home—the San Fernando Valley became her home. It would be too forced to have her rest back East, too improper—she belongs to the West. She will lie here."

One of the future visions that Fischer foretold of was played out in painful reality at Sherry's graveside. As in the vision, her mother showed me a small book— it was Sherry's diary. She said it was proper that I alone should have it. She coldly declared it unread, then, with her head tilted back in a poor attempt to counteract gravity on her tears, handed it over to me.

Sherry's mother, a pragmatic woman, held her opinion of her daughter deep inside her mouth. It was one that had taken her years to come to terms with, and at her burial, she forever silenced it and swallowed it down deep.

After the small funeral, her family went on their way back East and I felt as if I've been handed a torch, a duty of vigil over Sherry forever, as they would never, ever return.

There have been very few times in Los Angeles when I've felt I was right where I was supposed to be. Rarely have I taken a deep breath, looked around and said, "This is just right." The same goes for cemeteries. Even as I visit Sherry's grave today, I think, *this spot will never do for me*. Then again, I don't think any cemetery has the perfect spot to spend eternity.

All in all, I guess this spot for Sherry is just about as good as the next. Right over there is Buster Keaton, and over there Stan Laurel, and over there… someone unknown, once soft and sweet, and maybe as loving as Sherry Cleveland.

I haven't looked in the envelope that Sherry gave to me; I'm just putting one foot in front of the other these days, just doing as I'm told. I don't understand it, but Sherry instructed me not to open it until New York, so I must obey her in death, only because it's the last time that I can do something for her. Sherry's last living request is clearly and simply my duty.

There are days when sadness grips me, when the tally of wrongs and piles of problems grow full over my head, tamping down any forward progress to where I'm drawn back into worry or even capitulation. I'm not usually one to throw in the towel, but on these days, it's best that I don't fight at all. Today I'll just pray for the best, and hold on for dear mercy.

It's hard to think about what had become of Sherry, but she knew her fate and had sealed it herself. Sherry became one of them, but broke ranks in order to kill Vince.

I can't make heads or tails about how it all played out, especially when words like fate and destiny barge in and try to rearrange the macabre events into a more palatable fable. I won't have any of it because I don't have the capacity in either my soul or brain to comprehend what's gone on here, and can't see a time where I'll be able to tuck it away all neat and tidy.

I know I've had a change, I indeed have become a warrior, but I just can't let go of the fact that this should not have happened.

I'd have to say that the worst talent that I possess is the awful burden of being able to see people how they really should be, without faults, addictions, bad behavior etc. I can envision their optimum persona, without the corrupted flesh or tortured soul's interference.

In some people, this rotten attribute causes them to become a nag and a badger to their significant others, regularly after them to shape up. Most alcoholics and addicts usually have a person in their lives that knows how they really should behave and act. The person doing the correcting, nagging and hiding of bottles usually suffers as much or more than the alcoholic or addict and is usually just as ill.

I didn't badger or try to correct Sherry, for it would have stepped me up to a place where she would have trashed my heart—a place too close, and ultimately too far as well. Yes, I always saw the girl that Sherry should've and could've been, I just couldn't say much. I silently held her above all that she was, the blueprint of the Sherry that was never fully erected—clear, bright, happy Sherry.

It's September 1, and my love of the impossible, and passion for lost causes leads me to play summertime music on this day, and true to form, I take out my Beach Boy's records.

Brian Wilson expressed his sadness for a lost love in his haunting masterpiece entitled "Caroline, No." The withering vocal floats like a sad memory, over a ghostly reverbed accompaniment.

CHAPTER 17

THE SWIFT AND DEADLY

THE PHONE RINGS—IT'S Roberto. He tells me I did a wonderful job with Sherry's funeral, says some other niceties, and attempts to prepare me for what I already have prepared for myself.

We both know who the target is, and we discuss the risks and procedures involved. What's amazing to me is the lack of mysticism involved in all of this, for Roberto and his men handle it like a military operation, one with spiritual discipline and metered energy.

He tells me that my training had started the first day down at the river, that I have been watched and tested, and have performed wonderfully. It's actually really nice to hear some praise and to know that I've been doing pretty well at something. He tells me to continue using my instincts and thoughtful, honest emotions in order to carry this out successfully. He said that it was required—it was key.

"Close your eyes, amigo," Roberto tells me over the phone, then says he has something to show me.

"Did you show me the vision of Sherry killing Vince Shank, is that why I dreamt it?"

"Yes, Tru-man, I did, but lie back now, I need to show you some more things. Some very important things."

As if for dramatic effect the Santa Ana winds start to blow, rattling my windows as I lay my head down upon the pillow. He says some words or phrases that aren't in English, but ones that don't sound much like Spanish either. To be honest, I can't be sure about the language, but know that the words make perfect sense to me, and I begin to see.

The Santa Ana's blow my vision down into the office of Mr. Lawrence Fischer, and there's a young lady there with him involved in his typical debauchery. She stabs the cocaine on the mirror with a razor blade just a little too hard for the watchful eye of Lawrence, who senses some anger and rebellion in this girl. He physically sees her father's blood inside her veins causing her to resent him.

Her face is obscured, so I ask, "Is that her—is that Janice? If it is, I can't bear it Roberto."

"It is, and you must watch it, Tru-man. You can't vanquish him without this knowledge. As I told you, you need an emotional attachment, and you must be in control of these emotions. I am going to take you through the next ten hours, you will see and know all, but must remain here if our plan is going to work. Trust us, Tru-man, this is your final training and soon you will have a graduation. You can do it, amigo. We have faith in you."

With the help of his calming tone, I let go and let Roberto take me on a journey. The scene changes and I see Janice alone in a dirty hotel room, making phone calls, telling people to beware of the monster that is Lawrence Fischer. Her appearance is strung out and pale, but as the door to her room opens, it deteriorates further, bearing the burden of horror and fear.

Lawrence Fischer enters and is carrying a rope in his gloved left hand and with his right grabs Janice, pulling her down to her knees as he places the rope around her neck.

The bastard drags her to the center of the room and throws the rope over an ugly 1960s light fixture. She fights him viciously and violently kicks and claws at him, but his strength is more than sufficiently overpowering, and he begins to pull on the rope.

"Roberto, I beg of you, I can't take any more—my baby girl— that is my child."

Within seconds, the physical process of oxygen deprivation starts her on a journey to a place where she hears her mother Erica's call, just like she had when she was small and was beckoned home for dinner. Not being able to see her mother at first, Janice reaches out her hand into the darkness.

"Mommy, is that you?" she meekly calls, when

suddenly something quite strong snatches her hand and pulls her through—never to be heard from again.

If I weren't under Roberto's care, this vision would have been impossible to tolerate. He protects me and lets me sleep. I knew it was so, and saw myself there, realizing he was in the process of tempering my thoughts and hardening my heart for the battle that is to come. Of course, I'm devastated by what I saw, and my sleep will be fitful, but I'm resigned to the fact that I had to see it in order to continue and succeed with this mission.

*

I don't know how long I've been sleeping, but my visions go on over to Ron Carson's house. I'm right there in the cluttered, dusty living room watching him prepare and go through his morning.

I see Ron Carson arrange and evenly space the framed photographs of his lost daughter on the mantle, just as a priest would place candles on his altar. There is no time for outward tears today as his mind is set on what he has to do. To bolster support for his pending task, he systematically looks very deeply at each one, purposely driving home the hurt and masochistically twisting in the pain of each long-lost happy moment.

He always had his doubts on whether or not he was actually Erica's biological father, but at this moment it doesn't matter, not to him or even myself. His pain caused him to lose his faith to the point where he hadn't even gone to the old chapel at the mission for months; he even stopped believing that Erica and her daughter could be together, laughing in that place that mortals cannot comprehend.

I begin to realize that a bi-product of this strange event is to restore some serenity to this tortured man and give him back his life again.

"Very good, Tru-man... very good, for the holy man is the caring man," Roberto says.

To energize the anger he'll need for his chosen task, Ron Carson opens the lamp table drawer and takes out the letters and notes Janice had written to him and his departed wife throughout elementary school.

The Father's Day and Christmas cards on yellow lined paper prove to be too much, for as much of a warrior as he thinks he is, his inner dam breaks, and he pushes the drawer closed so as not to cause the colors on the precious artwork to run.

He tries to load his vintage army issued pistol with the .45 caliber cartridges that had been hanging around his gun safe for the better part of a decade, but has to make two attempts to do so. The first time he pulls back on the slide of the tricky weapon, it jams, twisting a bullet sideways out of the chamber. Clearing the foul, he snaps back the slide again and the next bullet thrusts forward, seating correctly. Then, tucking the large pistol into his jacket pocket, he sets out for the studio.

Driving down Interstate 5 towards the studio is quite non-eventful, and he doesn't even notice the group of four mattress trucks that cruise up slowly from behind. Little by little, Ron Carson and the men come together in an aviation style "finger-five" formation cruising southward with a deadly purpose.

Ron's driving becomes distracted as his mind begins drifting, first to the clouds above, then to a distant red tailed hawk and then to his niece, scantily clad, being pawed at and tormented by a monster of a man. He blinks his eyes and gulps, trying to dispel the disturbing daydream, his foot now metering unevenly on the gas pedal. He grimaces and concentrates on the road, trying to ignore the mental flak that's exploding in his thoughts.

Shaking his head, he attempts to straighten his car squarely in the center lane when another all too realistic vision bangs his mind with a powerful present-time punch of sick reality.

He sees his niece screaming in pain, and the perverse Fischer is laughing deeply and spitting down onto her naked writhing form. He tries to avert his eyes from the perverse view and in doing so, swerves his car dangerously and violently.

The valiant Roberto bellows a humanly incomprehensible, staccato word that snaps all of his angel brothers into swift action. Immediately the mattress trucks deftly and gracefully avert the collision, and like blue smoking ballerinas, swerve and circle around Ron Carson with loud mechanical whirring sounds emanating from within each truck.

The four trucks dance from lane to lane, over and over, around and around, like stunt driving acrobats, then, surrounding Ron Carson's car, they form an arrow-shaped, six-mattress-high barrier. Ron's vehicle rights itself and he softly regains control once more, falling back into his steady and straight mission of destruction. As his hallucinations stop, the four shepherding angels quietly guide him down to his exit.

*

My vision goes over the wall of the studio, pauses briefly at the top of the water tower then swoops on down to Fischer's office. Seeing through others' eyes, I get to know my enemy and watch while the entire plan comes together. I experience the deep darkness of Fischer, but can also feel his confusion and weakness.

Fischer knows his communication has been interrupted, and he curses, not unlike a campy movie villain. Courtney is there and begins to get a little nervous—she'd never seen him in such a state. He was always so sure of himself, so full of the evil-cool that was once so very attractive to this young aspiring actress. He was the culmination of everything she thought she'd ever wanted, but now seeing the cracks, the angst and the flaws of this demon, her wants, like him, were beginning to unravel.

She heard about Vince Shank being killed and knew that this had to be a significant blow to Fischer, not because he mourned the man, but because he felt he might be next. The studio walls were large and protective, but once breached, there weren't many places you could run, for the same walls that could keep others out, could also trap you in.

She tells him that she's stepping outside for a cigarette, but he doesn't hear her, as he's busy calling security, making sure that Ron Carson doesn't get on the lot. As she often does, she thinks of her uncle and her cousin, and the simple life they had together. Sure it was boring and could never be as wild as the nights on the town, the private screenings, the celebrities, the coke and yes, the sex—but where were her movie roles? He had promised over and over that she'd be a star.

She's looked plainly at herself in the mirror of late; she's looked close and deep. She's no longer an innocent child, and has become a woman—and that woman doesn't like what she sees. Her uncle raised her to see things truly—in his own common man way, and now that the attraction of Hollywood and fame has shown its ugly face, she's finally able and opened minded enough to be approached.

For a while, the mirror had shown her the empress, the one who was without reproach, the one flying above all the commoners and their silly rules, and then here under the shadow of the water tower, as if wiping all the false glitter paint from the glass, an important voice re-introduces itself to this lovely young lady.

"Hi, it's me, Dennis."

The young man, the one that she'd met previously

in the commissary, steps into the light between her and the water tower.

"Sorry to bug you, I don't know if you remember me, but I'm still kind of lost. Can you tell me how to get to the commissary from here? I want to try one of those green teas."

She looks at him transfixed and can't believe that someone with so much charm could be such a nerd. Clearly, he's an actor, a gorgeous actor with a face that should be on the cover of a cereal box, but there's something wrong—he's too together, too clean for Hollywood.

He's so neat and clean that she thinks he could use some dirtying up, but then realizes if that happens, he'd then look like all the other young men on the lot, the young men with giant gaudy watches and greasy hair matted down under wool caps, the ones that say, "it's all good" and "right on" with the pretentious questioning inflection.

Clearing her mind of the darkness, then clearing her throat, she says:

"Oh yeah, the commissary—just around that sound-stage there, make a left, then walk straight, you'll run right into it. Hey, are you going to accost someone that wants to sit quietly and drink their green tea?"

Dennis smiles softly.

"Glad you remember me, can I buy you a late lunch?"

She just stares at him coldly, but he is undaunted and presses her.

"Okay, well then how about you come along to the commissary and just sit with me for a while?"

Courtney just blinks her eyes at him like she's sending a secret Morse code of playful annoyance.

Seeing that he isn't making much headway, he exchanges his upbeat tone for a more truthful approach.

"Look, I still really don't know anyone here, and well... you're just lovely."

She's taken aback by his charming candor. It's not the LA way to risk all with a bold statement. Words are normally parsed or indefinite here, and conclusions or passionate truths are far too risky for simple conversations, besides, you don't get many chances from the bottom up in a town like Hollywood, where even the top men hedge their bets.

It seems today that this bold man's gambit has paid off, for after hearing his sweet, simple words, she softly smiles, and her old San Fernando smile alights on her face.

"Welcome to Hollywood, Mister Noob."

As she says those words she feels like a spell has been broken. Her body feels heavy, like when you rise out of a long hot bath. Her mind feels elevated, yet weak and out of sorts, like when you have a hangover.

From the first day she entered the world of Lawrence Fischer, she had lost her sense of self. She became one of his soulless followers, forever waiting for him to pull her through his purgatory of promises and finally bestow a real life on her. She now understands that it was never to be, and her real life was the one that she'd left behind.

As strange as it sounds, these few kind words from this handsome young man have finally pushed her past her own tipping point. She's starting to realize that underneath the layers of faux-affluent, phony-actress nonsense, right here under the water tower, is a real woman, capable of honest mature thought. This is her reawakening—this is her epiphany.

She looks up to the tower, and smiles an even larger smile now, the kind that hasn't broken on her face for quite some time. Yes, she does like him, and knows that there's no need for her cultured sulky-cool behavior with this man. Somewhere below his eyes is a smile that she feels more than sees. He has a graceful meter to his movements, not unlike a dancer, he even smells good, with inviting subtle cologne that mixes pleasantly with the hot summer air.

It is indeed a good idea to go with Dennis and escape the coming meltdown that's sure to erupt from Fischer, for she knows that if she's anywhere in Lawrence's proximity, she'll suffer the same sadistic treatment he dishes out whether he's aroused or angry.

So taking a deep breath, she stands up and takes a very large step away with Dennis, pushing against a weakening physical barrier that appears to be holding her back. Dennis senses it, so he gently holds her elbow and softly grips her shoulder like a nurse guiding a recovering patient.

Courtney's gate is at first tenuous, but then she brightens and picks up the pace as the bonds placed on her by Fischer diminish with each succeeding step.

*

The Mattress Men land Ron Carson safely down on the street right outside the rear studio gate. Ron is badly shaken. Although he doesn't know exactly why, he knows that he's in good hands and doesn't ask where they're from, or why they have come to his aid.

The unassuming angels had brought him into a gentle understanding without using any words, their silent powers abridged questions that would naturally come into anyone's mind, when four old pickup trucks piled high with mattresses happen to rescue you from disaster.

"We're calling Tru-man for you," Roberto tells him. "He's the one who needs to do what is in your heart, for your daughter. You must go home. You'll lose if you go in, and Courtney needs you alive. Go, Ron Carson, there are no more tragedies allowed for this bastard, Fischer."

Ron instinctively knows they're right, and that he really isn't a killer. He has anger that surpasses the mission's need for a professional coolness, an anger that assuredly would bring disaster. Yes, the best thing he can do right now, is to go home.

He once again realizes that he is indeed a religious man, and that all his years spent at the old chapel have led him to this very encounter. This is something that he had prayed for—this is his holy moment. Ron stares incredulously at them, then, slowly makes the sign of the cross as he turns back towards his car.

Roberto and his men watch him drive away, and then quickly prepare for battle.

On his way home, Ron Carson heads up Lankershim Boulevard, makes a left onto Riverside Drive and is about to get on the freeway when he sees a very pretty redheaded woman standing next to her car, waving at him for assistance. Being a classic car man, he cannot resist a look at the very singular automobile—it's a gorgeous 1939 Lincoln Zephyr V-12.

*

When I awoke from these visions, a bit late this morning, I indeed had seen all, and was aware that I was about to go into action.

Sitting at my breakfast table, I look over at a photo of Sherry and I taken a few years back on one of our last day trips we took up to Santa Barbara. Standing out on the docks we asked a passer-by to take a picture of us.

I remember the feeling I had when I moved in close and put my arm around her waist. It was a good fit, so right, comfortable and natural that it put an invisible check next to one of the silent questions of my manhood—the physical answer that spoke volumes without so much as a whisper.

All of a sudden, like the photos in Fischer's office, Sherry's image turns her head and looks at me square on. I'm not afraid, for my heart burns with love and sadness. I touch the photograph and tell her silently that I love her. Deep down, I know that she hears me, and it brings me great comfort, and just in time, great courage.

My cell phone rings.

Roberto is calling me asking for my assistance, I knew the call was coming and am resigned to it. I'm their man. I'm the executioner, and for the first time in my adult life, I feel very important and worthy.

"I'll be there soon," are the only words I say to him.

Ron Carson was a red herring, a clever deception played expertly by Roberto and his men, achieved wonderfully in no small part by Ron's burning passion to avenge Janice. Ron's dark desire is what Fischer sensed, but more than that, it was all that he could see.

Lawrence Fischer was blinded by his desire to keep Courtney away from her uncle Ron, and also by his incorrect assessment of me as a failure. Fischer doesn't fear me at all, and Roberto has used his arrogant complacency as the key to our advantage.

Roberto has been brilliant, and along with the other angels, has let it all play out, right up to the very gates of the studio. Still, there will be high paranoia at that gate today, and if I'm to slip in, it will have to be inside a Trojan horse, a V-12 Trojan horse.

As if anticipating my next move, Jane honks her unmistakable vintage horn in front of my place, garnering attention from many of the howling dogs in the neighborhood.

I walk out, get in the passenger seat, and shut the door.

"Are you here to kill me or help me?" I ask her.

She turns to me and in her hand is a large pistol pointed right at my stomach. With a flair for the dramatic, Jane takes about a three second pause before deftly flipping the pistol around, handing the familiar army issued .45 to me, grips first.

"Ron Carson is not the man to carry this today—you are," she says.

I have a lot of questions for Jane Axton. Whether she's with them or us, I feel confused and angry knowing that she's obviously been part of this affair for the entire time.

*

Fischer paces his office and makes several more calls to security for updates and lookouts. With no new information forthcoming, his anger and rare nervousness turn his interest toward finding Courtney, for he knows that she's still the bait.

As he leaves his office, he actually feels numb—no homing sensation as to his desired prey, no power to lure back even so much as a hungry pet. He feels nothing from Courtney, nothing from the guards, and nothing from the backlot itself. The passers-by are not of their usual demeanor for they all have strange softer faces—some even smile at him.

It seems that his minions, those that could sweep up a storm of confusion and trouble, have now disbanded, quiet in the universe. Although alone and weakened, he is still astute enough to know that this temporary shift in power is directly correlated to the coming onslaught, and that it is time to retreat to his office and prepare for the attack.

*

Jane looks down and shuts me into the trunk of her car, and I wonder if I'd just glimpsed my last daylight. It's hot inside, and the trunk smells of gas fumes and musty age. Mercifully, our travel is short, and I feel much better hearing that we've pulled up to the security gate. As much as I want out, I know that if I make a noise, the operation will be over. I hear some muffled conversation, then a stage laugh from Jane, before we're slowly rolling once again.

The cooler air is quite welcome as Jane releases me from the trunk. I check Ron's pistol, and turn off its safety as she and I walk swiftly and resolutely towards Fischer's office. The last remaining doubt about which team Jane is playing for is being stamped out with each firm step towards the target. Her face looks quite different—it's as cold as winter steel, with the blue-dead look of a trained assassin.

As we get closer, my feet start to plod a bit heavier, signaling Fischer has already started his mind tricks. He may have been fooled for a while, but the bastard now surely knows that I'm coming for him.

"Try to keep up, Tru, you must try as hard as you can," Jane tells me. Her voice is deadly serious.

I summon all of my strength and pause to look lovingly at Jane, seeking to resurrect any evidence of our passion, but she averts my prying look. Arriving at his office entrance, our eyes meet briefly. Sadly, I see and feel nothing familiar.

Knowing it's time to discard all personal feelings and get on with the task at hand, I swallow, take a deep breath—then swing around and violently kick the son-of-a-bitch's door open.

It had an effect because I could swear I saw Lawrence Fischer flinch a little. He stands up behind his desk and slowly steps towards the center of the room.

"The loser returns!" he bellows.

The unusually loud volume is my second clue as to his rattled state. I turn back to look at Jane, but find no one—she's gone.

Fischer senses my distraction and tries to use his powers on me, attempting to make me as delusional as I was at our last meeting. I do see some nasty things very quickly, almost like viewing a defective movie projector running film past faulty sprockets.

As I begin to walk towards him with the .45 pistol pointed straight at his omnipotent head, I see Sherry and him in a hellish embrace, which makes me walk faster, Courtney in a sexual position, which makes me cock the hammer, and the beast himself strangling and hanging my beautiful daughter Janice in the motel room—which makes me pull the goddamned trigger.

His visions obviously had some effect—they stirred my anger, thus causing the first bullet to miss, slightly right. His face goes nearly white with shock, and I steady my hand and remember what my dad told me as a young boy in my pistol training.

Hold your breath and just gently squeeze, don't jerk the trigger.

I listen and obey, but grimace as I hear a sickening *clank*.

The gun has jammed.

The second bullet is turned sideways, sticking out of the chamber just like it had when Ron first loaded it.

Fischer's blood flows back into his face, and thinking his powers have been restored, he laughs and slowly starts towards me.

I stand frozen, thinking that this is the ultimate joke of my failed life. I must have been kidding myself to think that I could actually be a successful devil hunter. Once again, the feel-sorry-for-himself Truman is coming in loud-and-clear.

"You just screwed it up once again, Truman! You *are* a loser. Losers die."

Lawrence Fischer resumes his hellish demeanor and comes closer and closer. My legs are now immobilized as his powers are growing rapidly once again. Since I've tried and failed to kill him, he's now able to return the deed, and according to the rules, I'm now no longer protected. These are to be my last moments on earth.

"Mister!"

The sound of her voice from behind me reaches my brain before my ears have a chance to process it. I turn to see that Courtney has entered the room along with her new friend. She deftly throws me her small revolver, the same gun she had brandished at me some months ago when I picked her up hitchhiking. I snatch the gun out of the air and take aim.

The sound in my head goes from a roaring cacophony of gruesome illusions, to a loud bang followed by a small, ugly gasp from Fischer's mouth as the .38 bullet pierces his forehead.

Fischer falls backward, and hits the floor.

It's not the same as it appears on television or in movies—it's a very ghastly thing with no music score to sweep over it, no edits or fade-outs to avert your eyes or hide the physical mess. It demands your attention, and it certainly has all of mine.

Suddenly, as if they were all hiding, Roberto and his men calmly and quickly enter the office. Roberto goes over to Fischer and feels his pulse.

"His heart is still beating... hurry."

His command is directed to Dennis, Courtney's new friend. He looks very familiar to me.

Jane walks into the office, and I'm very glad to see her.

"I'm sorry, Truman, but you had to do it yourself," she says quite coolly.

She joins the others as they immediately go about cleaning the room placing furniture in particular spots and picking up the jammed .45 caliber pistol. They all behave as if they've done this a hundred times.

Jane gently takes Courtney's revolver from my shaking hand and wipes it clean, then places it in Fischer's twitching hand. Courtney's friend Dennis reaches into his own jacket pocket and pulls out what looks like a bag of cocaine, dumping some down upon the desk and placing some in Fischer's open mouth.

Inside his jacket, I can't help notice an LAPD badge. My shock lessening, I now recognize him as the detective that was kind to Sherry the day she was arrested. The same detective I suspected had known Roberto, and had called me with the news of Sherry's death.

Detective Dennis Vega brutally holds Fischer's bloody mouth closed, then checks it to see if the cocaine was absorbed. It was, and I watch the last grimaces of struggle leave Lawrence Fischer's body.

The stage is set, and with the demon now finally confirmed dead, we begin to leave the office. Roberto is the last to leave, and in backing out of the room, he genuflects several times. There's a strange flash of golden-yellow light as Roberto makes the sign of the cross, just inside the entry. Jane and Detective Dennis Vega also make the sign of the cross, and close their eyes as Roberto prays.

"We walk with Blessed Padres, Junipero Serra and Juan Crespi, we will work for the meek and sew flowers in your valley, forever and ever. Amen."

With that, Roberto closes the door to Lawrence Fischer's office.

Now I know—now it's all making sense. The only angels that would plan a bloody horror such as this would be the very swift and deadly type—archangels.

Roberto and his Mattress Men all look at me very seriously as we walk slowly towards the water tower. Armando playfully punches my shoulder and smiles. In their eyes, I see admiration and pride, and in Roberto's big smile I see a "thank you."

I've never been in traditional combat, but now know what it's like to share that very special bond with fellow warriors and because of it, will love them all forever. We nod to each other as they peel off and walk down one of the smaller alleys on the lot. Then, with a final wave, they disappear around a corner.

"I'll take Courtney home to her uncle," Detective Dennis Vega says.

Dennis knows what he was charged to do, for he too was given an important letter, and held it in his jacket pocket. I saw it and was relieved that I was not the only one recruited.

Who knew how many more devils were left in The San Fernando Valley? It didn't seem to matter to him. It was quite obvious from Detective Vega's bold and sure manner that these hidden dangers were no match for his diligent purpose. Some would call it faith, but I guess that would depend on the amount of belief you possess.

Courtney looks haunted, but also somewhat relieved to be leaving the clutches of the lot. She glances up at the Tower, and begins to feel cleansed, thinking to herself how much she's missed the warmth of her cousin, and how nice it will be to see her uncle once more. She feels lucky to be escaping and swears in this moment that the rest of her life will be very different.

Before she gets into the car, she stops and glances around the lot, knowing in her heart that she'll never return. Then, she tosses these feelings away just like a crushed paper cup and smiles at Detective Vega as he closes her passenger door. He gets in the driver's side, and she looks over at him as he adjusts his jacket and feels for his gun. She'll have many questions for the handsome man, but now all she wants to do is go home.

"This must have been hard for you both," Detective Dennis Vega tells us.

Jane and I walk around to his side of the car.

"Take care, both of you," he adds.

I acknowledge his verbal stroke with a grimaced smile, the kind you show when you can't process emotion and need to put on a brave face. As I watch them drive off, I know it is also time for us to leave. Jane then motions for me to turn around.

"Someone is here to see you," she says.

Turning around, I see Asher Corrigan standing directly under the water tower. He put his hands in the air backed with a coy smile as if to say, "Well, what about me?"

I smile, turn back around, grab Jane by the hand, and as we move towards her car, shout back to him:

"Asher, I release you!"

He laughs and shakes himself out for a second or two, and then slowly turns back into the lot. He seems light in his step and relieved, walking straight, then turning left, then right, finally falling from view, enveloped by the giant soundstages.

I didn't have the strength to climb back into Jane's trunk, and luckily it's just fine for us, for we smoothly cruise past the unusually empty exit gate. Meshing into the snarl of the late afternoon valley traffic, all of the day's violent images and sounds begin swirling around in my head.

Though the ride home is short, I tightly hold a thousand miles of mystery deep inside. As we arrive in front of my condo, Jane also seems lost, and just stares straight ahead.

"Jane, I have so many questions."

She finally turns her head towards me, but remains completely silent.

CHAPTER 18

VOYEURS FROM THE BINS

KILLING SOMEONE, EVEN someone as horrible as Lawrence Fischer, isn't an easy event to set aside once it's completed. You don't just take a nap and forget about it. My exhaustion combined with my nagging confusion about Jane prevented me from seeing her over the last few days. She didn't call, and that's a good thing, and though I've longed to see her, I didn't want my feelings for her get in the way of finding out the whole truth.

This morning I feel that it's high time I get some answers, so I amble up Lankershim Boulevard to Trader John's, and find her standing there behind the cash register, patiently waiting for the few remaining record collectors in the San Fernando Valley to wander in and purchase something.

"I want it all, I want to know everything. I want to move on, one way or the other," I say.

She slowly reaches across the counter, and presses

my hand, still bearing a good amount of the captured-spy straight face that I saw on the lot the other day. It almost looks as if she is another person posing as Jane, like there is someone else behind the mask.

"There's not much to tell. I was contacted just as you were. I was recruited just as you were. I certainly didn't think I would develop these feelings for you either, Truman."

"Why did they choose you?" I ask.

She stares at me in cold silence, and I can't tell if she is angry or afraid. Pushing past me, she comes out from behind the counter and looks as if she's going to walk out of the store, but then stops at the door, locks it, and flips the sign in the window to "closed."

"Jane, did you hear what I said?"

She turns to look at me, pulls down the old shade on the door, and closes the blinds in the two front windows that flank the entrance. With the late afternoon valley sun now dimmed in her shop, I'm apprehensive about what may come next.

She quickly turns and walks towards me with her eyes downcast and her hands rising up. My legs stiffen as my body prepares for physical defense—thankfully there's no need.

Our embrace leads first to soft kisses and gentle caresses. Then with our eyes wide open, and spurred on by the novel surroundings, we let our searching knees, hands, and mouths, escalate our late afternoon rendez-vous, pitching it up to a raw explosive encounter.

In a store filled with the world's greatest music, we listen to nothing but each other's hungry utterances, while Nat King Cole and Beach Boys records, peek like voyeurs from their bins, the brilliance in their grooves hushed for this glorious occasion.

Our passion bursts and unwraps so much of the tension that been building between us. We giggle like school kids when one of her regular customers, obviously in need of a vinyl fix; knocks on the door repeatedly, before leaving a dejected and disappointed collector.

I realize there could be passion and laughter with Jane, and I want to go to the next place with her, I want the usual joys and problems that all relationships have— I want her oddities, her moods, and her mysteries.

Since the death of Sherry, and the elimination of Fischer, I've prayed for some normalcy in my life. Time and again, all the answers to those prayers seem to have Jane's name attached to them, and because of that, I feel it's time to tidy up my manhood and gather in all the childish behaviors that keep me aloof, adrift, and alone. I want Jane to know that I'll do this for her, and need to find the courage to tell her.

*

September is moving on, but the valley is still sweltering. I thought about taking her up to Carmel or the central coast wine region; however, that would require some planning, driving, getting cash out of the bank, reservations, reservation numbers, talking to people… in other words, it would require function.

After what I'd been through, I'm totally dysfunctional, a shattered heap, relegated to simple one word responses and needing only the basic necessities. I merely want Jane to hold me, alone, quiet, away from all demons, angels or anything normal that fits in between.

We decide to keep it simple with a stay at home dinner and an evening drive up into the Hollywood Hills. Winding our way up Laurel Canyon in Jane's more than capable Lincoln, we reach the summit, and make a right turn onto Mulholland Drive.

Coming upon a clearing, we begin to see the beautiful twinkling lights of the valley below, and are amazed at all the people, cars, and life that have been jammed into this finite space.

We pull off to an overlook, and feel just like high school sweethearts, nervous that a cop will come along and cite us for loitering. However, since I've recently shot a man, seen ghosts, and bid farewell to a dear friend—I think I can hold and kiss this woman, without having to worry too much about any petty consequences.

Jane is as ravishing as ever in her simple way and leaning over, she holds me as no woman has held me in many years. I want to tell her how I feel right now, that despite all of our fears and confusion, despite the lingering questions, tell her that she has truly become my life's choice.

"Sometimes you must love what you can't understand."

Right on cue, she whispers words that seem to sum up the moment, if not our whole relationship. Such words from a gorgeous woman are to be paid attention to, and the transmission that is my heart misses two shifts on the way from affection to deep passion. My declaration—will have to wait for another day.

*

Her eager uncle brings his long lost niece out for a simple breakfast. They're sitting in the local Denny's, without many words passing between them. Courtney looks nothing like the leather-panted hitchhiking evil-one that ran around with Lawrence Fischer, in fact, quite the opposite.

"Don't you want some black pepper on your eggs? Gotta have black pepper on eggs," her uncle asks.

She looks like a lost little girl, one that needs nourishment, love and attention. Her uncle passes her the black pepper for her eggs and she nods in agreement, looking somewhat uncomfortable in this simple setting. Her mouth is full of toast and eggs, but still she recognizes her uncle's gesture with a warm smile.

"I want to say I'm sorry, Uncle. I'm so very sorry for what we did, I thought it'd be different."

He knew that his niece would never replace Janice, his little girl that would never come home, but his path has been chosen, and he'll walk it well. He'll do his best to raise this girl for the next year or two before she once again goes out into the world, and vows that the next time she leaves, she'll go out a better person.

Thanks to the archangels, Ron has regained his manhood, and come home to the old chapel. He looks at his niece and knows that he's right where he's supposed to be.

"Welcome home sweetheart."

Courtney bursts into tears that drip down onto her plate.

*

Roberto has a new friend. She's new to the group and very, very beautiful. In his line, there has never been time or room for romantic feelings. What has been entrusted to him, his duty, is a never ending quest for greatness, so he doesn't know if it's permitted, but he's smitten—his heart is doing flips. He tries his best to hide his former gang tattoos, the ones he got years ago for a special mission. He figured this lovely lady wouldn't like them at all.

Roberto could hide his feelings for her, as she knew he would, as it wasn't his place to love her right now, as she would pine for Truman into eternity. Roberto, in turn, would hide his into the same.

"I want to welcome you to us, miss… you are very much needed here," Roberto tells her sternly, hiding his affection.

She stares like a newborn babe at this large man.

She can hardly think past her giddy fascination with her new feelings and circumstances. She brushes back the platinum blonde hair revealing her now drug-free, clear blue eyes, and touches her familiar cross that hangs just above her breast.

The pickup truck will change appearance; it's been a hand cart, then a buggy, then a Model T truck, but whatever it becomes in the future, it will forever smoke on down the Coldwater Canyon, across the Ventura Freeway, rounding back off the Burbank hills again and again, 'round and 'round, like an old-school California skateboarder forever patrolling the San Fernando Valley.

*

Jane kisses me again, and unbeknownst to me; begins to hope for the possibility of our life together. She silently prays, nearly begging for her change, when she is softly reminded who she really is, what she is doing here, and the worst of it; what she has to do in the next few days.

*

Courtney misses her cousin so very much. She's grateful to have her uncle, and sees the pain he holds deep down in the newer lines on his face. She also knows that the time they have left together will be short, and mostly ceremonial, for she's grown up and will soon find love, and in spite of her lack of fame, true happiness.

Detective Dennis Vega will loom large in her future.

The moment he met her on the lot was a planned one, but her feelings for the young LAPD detective are true, and he in turn also feels that he's found his life's partner in Courtney and has promised that no one will ever hurt her again.

*

I am awakened by a knock on my door. The fabulous scent of Jane's unmistakable perfume still hangs heavy in my bedroom and I vaguely remember her leaving around dawn. I open the door and find another note on my doormat, and once again it's a letter from me, to me.

As with the first one, I'm wary of who sent it and why, and just like the first one, it has my attention, for the facts contained therein could not be known by anyone else.

> *Hurry, stop what you're doing, you need to be here by tomorrow. If you still don't believe that I'm you, then dig this: You never told anyone about the time you floated a foot off the ground for about thirty seconds when you were nine years old.*

> *Be here by tomorrow morning or we're dead. Get to Burbank Airport and get on the plane — come to this address and bring the photos.*

I've never told a soul about my levitation event, but its inclusion in the letter and the fact that it also mentions the photos, are all I need for verification. The note doesn't mention it, but I've been counting, and I am now certain that the last two devils, numbers five and six, will be faced on this trip.

I call Jane and tell her I can't take this trip alone. The request alone defines my love for her, and I hope her acceptance is the practical admission of hers in return. When all this business is done, I'd like to spend some time there, maybe see some Broadway shows; have some great dinners, stroll through Central Park.

New York in the fall... it's the perfect place for a marriage proposal.

*

We enter the airport parking garage and being that the lower spaces are full, we drive around and around until we finally find a spot on the rooftop level. We pull into a space that has a wonderful vista of the valley to the south, and notice that directly ahead is the studio's water tower. The tower's red light is beating a rhythmic message not unlike a lighthouse viewed from the sea.

Fear of the unknown always creates more anxiety, and Jane's quiet demeanor isn't helping things. Jane stares at the tower, and appears distracted, then grabs me around my neck, turns her face sideways and hugs me very deeply.

"I'm afraid," she says.

"Don't be afraid," I say. I then show her the small, unopened envelope Sherry had given to me the day she died.

"It's a package of photos," I tell her. "Sherry told me to be sure to bring these to New York. Hold them for me—I'll carry our bags in."

We sit for a while at gate number twenty-three, waiting for our flight. On the way in we passed a large machine that sells fresh roses, and I thought it would be nice to surprise Jane with one.

"I've got to go the men's room," I tell her.

Jane grabs my hand firmly, pulls me close and kisses me tenderly. She slowly releases her grip and touches my cheek as I back away.

"Don't worry, Jane. Watch the bags, I'll be right back."

I quickly walk down the main concourse a few gates towards the flower machine. I think back all those years ago to Erica, standing here alone at this airport, welcoming me with a single rose and wonder if this is the same machine that she got hers from.

I choose a yellow one—a luscious, lively color that seems to suit Jane just right. The rose is large and beautiful and still has moisture on its petals, and I can't help but wonder how far it's traveled just to sit in this refrigerated box. At ten dollars for a single rose, I surmise that most customers are either smitten boyfriends deep in lust, or guilt-ridden bastards crawling back from their secrets in Las Vegas.

I walk back to our gate but do not see Jane seated by our bags. Wondering where she might have gone, I look further along the empty concourse and see an elderly woman looking at me, standing just about two gates down.

The woman lifts her hand and softly waves, and though waving back is a natural reaction, an eerie, frightful awe prevents me from doing so. I begin walking towards this lady with an unholy fear that governs down my pace. Then, a burning sense of reality unlocks my legs and the speed of my gate increases with each successive footstep.

As I get closer, the woman recoils, and puts her hand to her mouth as if to stifle emotion or tears, just like my Erica used to do. She's a beautiful woman dressed peculiarly in clothes from the nineteen-thirties.

Her face is very familiar—she looks just like Erica, then Jane, and then Erica again—like the woman from the photo, the old photo from Jane's store, the woman from the town of Lankershim.

Nearly panicked, and now at a full run, I scream out for Erica, then Jane, my voice rudely bouncing off all the hard surfaces in the terminal, then with each slow motion reflection of my echoing scream, Jane/Erica washes out and dims slightly, little by little until the echo and her image completely and quietly disappear.

"Last call sir," the steward prods.

I realize that I must have dozed off in my seat while waiting at the gate. Sherry's photo envelope is there resting atop my carry-on. I get up, grip my rolling bag and tuck the envelope of photos into my jacket's inner pocket. Then, after a painful final look down the concourse, I become resigned to the reality of what has happened and slowly move towards the gate, reluctantly leaving her yellow rose on the seat behind.

I hope that she'll come back for it; I hope to buy her many more for the rest of my life. She is the island of my forties——my rest stop in a desert of uninterested parties and old memories. I don't care what or who she is, I just hope that she had a very good reason to leave, and will come back to me for the very best reason of all.

The steward calls again, and though my heart is breaking, I now know that I have become someone else. I am no longer a hapless writer, waiting for a job. I am now an important man with an important task to fulfill, and this woman's disappearance, whomever she was, is just an unfortunate part of the mission.

It's been a long strange summer, and now that the fall is upon us, it's fitting that I've been summoned back to the place where the fall lives to its fullest. I walk into the plane a broken-hearted, though resolute man—a man that really doesn't care if anyone notices.

The plane shuffles slowly, heading towards the runway. I look back to the terminal and see it as a large box, with my dreams wrapped quietly and invisibly inside.

Wisdom gives us the knowledge to know when we must wait and be patient, but if we are truly wise, we will use that idle time to summon the bravery required, to accept our present situation.

CHAPTER 19

313

I MOVE ON WITH the mechanical stiffness of a man who has removed his heart in order to do what he has to do. The flight is uneventful, but being a nervous flyer, my hands are stiff from gripping the arms of the seat too tightly during our descent.

I look to several other faces seeking to find an ally in traveler's angst, but come up with blank stares. It's especially glaring on this flight filled with twenty-somethings, as the wires that connect any spark of interest from people their age to mine, has long been disconnected. Wise people tell me my fear of flying is caused by my desire for control, the wiseass inside me knows that it's not the flying that I'm afraid of, it's the crashing.

As we land at JFK, the world seems different; I can almost immediately feel the East Coast vibe seeping into the plane. It doesn't come in the windows, or through the engines or doors, it comes in through the people who are predisposed to receiving it, leaving the others as mere tourists who will bring home stories of bad manners and rude behavior. I see it in the flight attendants attitude, the way the guy next to me stiffens, and in the captain's more hurried announcements.

New York is a tectonic shift away from the attitudes and customs of Los Angeles and the San Fernando Valley, there is a palpable difference in the way things are said, done and experienced. Here, even the birds on the runway seem different.

In Los Angeles, things seem to present themselves much more plainly and successfully. Things seem defined and bright and are addressed with a bit more weight—things just stand out more. I don't think it's the fact that Los Angeles is the entertainment capital of the world, rather I think it is the natural chemistry of the environment.

The mountains say, "Here I am," and you notice. The billboards say, "Look at me," and you look. Los Angeles is a land where car dealers become television princes and where strange nothings can become everything.

Back East, things are more camouflaged by the confusion of the seasons, the closed doors, the suspicious alienation of success and the weight of European ancestral behaviors. In Los Angeles if you say it the right way, you are it. In the East, when you say it, most likely you'll be interrupted.

My re-entry into New York City is christened with

a downpour of rain, and although it is not the autumn reception I'd hoped for, it's a perfect counterpoint to the never-ending monotonous and steady sun beat of Los Angeles. I take a cab from JFK airport to the address I'd received in the letters. When I arrive at the location on East Seventy-first Street, the rain has finally subsided but is replaced by a stiff, chilly wind.

I stand in front of my appointed building, number 313, and just stare at its entrance. There are feelings coming upon me that somehow I am indeed very familiar with this place.

"Impossible," I mutter, shaking wise with myself. I know that I've never set foot inside this address. Still, I'm even more nervous than when I first stepped into Lawrence Fischer's office. Fischer was what I expected to find there, but here; God only knows.

New York is so very real to me, so alive and present, so unveiled and raw. It was my home for years, and although the streets and neighborhoods are extremely familiar to my eyes, my heart has long since left here. This granite island has been traipsed for centuries by countless scores of people that are long since dead and buried, stacked three and four high deep in the cemeteries along the Long Island Expressway.

I myself have many relatives buried out there whose graves I have never even seen. They walked these streets, day after day, working then falling into their dark little apartments, down into their book-nook lives. They had galley kitchens, miserable long hot summers, and unfortunately for them, the only way they got off this island was in a coffin.

I am less of an actualized man here than I was on the West Coast, although I was indeed constructed here, not only by my parents, but molded and honed by the businesses, women, friends and enemies that have made me who I am. Now, like an abandoned bird's nest, my former home holds nothing for me.

Standing here, trying to summon the courage to enter the apartment, I feel a separation in what was once reality, and what has become reality, and in that, a futility and sadness grips me. Once you live here, it's hard to be a tourist in New York City. Gone are the old friends, business connections, even the girls, long since married off, in Jersey, Long Island or elsewhere. It is indeed an empty experience to visit the past—for in the past we are ghosts, we touch nothing and change nothing.

As I enter the building, the number address above the door begins to change. The two three's in the 313 grow mirror images of themselves forming two number eights, and the address becomes 818 East Seventy-first Street right in front of my eyes. I remember Roberto telling me about the "split infinity" of the San Fernando Valley area code—I have this funny feeling that I was about to find out its meaning.

Through the double doors and down a few steps, I enter into the sparsely decorated art deco building. There she is, sitting on the curved couch tucked into the corner of the lobby. Over her head is a fairly well painted mural of a man; Mr. Lenox, of Lenox Hill fame, working the fields of his farm, plowing what once was East Seventy-first Street.

The counterpoint of this bucolic scene eventually morphing into the definitive Upper East Side urban neighborhood could not trump my surprise at seeing the face that sits smiling so softly before me. The Six Devils letter buzzes in my pocket once more, and as I look at the name next to number five, I hear her familiar voice.

"Hello, Truman."

"Mae," I say calmly. I try not to exhibit too much confusion or surprise.

"Tru, Tru, Tru," she says shaking her head in feigned disapproval, "you could've been very wealthy, and stayed on the inside circle. You could have dined with the elite, worked your way into quite a lofty position, but you screwed it."

"So it's been you the whole time, Mae. You've been behind all of this."

Mae laughed hard, with nearly the power of a twenty-two year old.

"You think I'm behind all of this? You are so very naïve, I'm merely a manager. I had my job to do with you Truman, and you really messed me over.

"So I got you in trouble—isn't that something?"

"Yes, but not as much as you're in son... and put

that silly letter away, those mattress trucks have no power here."

Mae then takes a deep breath, and calms herself down.

"Truman—I tell you what; today's your lucky day, I've seen fit to get you one last chance at true redemption."

She points to a ground floor apartment across the lobby, number 1-F. I find her words and gesture so frightening, that they actually surpass the feeling of shock at having been duped all these years. Summoning the courage of my forefathers, I resist caving to fear.

"Mae, I have stared down and faced two very evil men in the last few months. Whatever you have in store for me behind that door, can't be any more evil or challenging than they were."

The lights in the lobby start to dim, and I can swear that I feel wind and smell hay. Indeed, the painting of Mr. Lenox in the large mural above Mae's head starts to move. He is walking with his plow digging up the earth, and from underneath the dirt, snakes, rats and giant bugs come running, jumping and biting up his legs, around his chest and atop his head. As if he feels nothing, he keeps on plowing as they eat him alive—his head and body quickly devoured with his arms dropping the plow as they're ripped apart and torn off.

With that, the letter now in my back pocket, buzzes once more. I have an upsetting and foreboding feeling in my stomach, not unlike the permanent revulsion to a particular food once you've been sickened by it. It's time for the last one—it's time for number six.

Mae begins laughing again, a sickeningly deep laugh as if her voice is being digitally lowered an octave or two. I'm turned around and away from this horror as if on a turntable, and I begin to float very slowly towards apartment 1-F.

The door slowly opens without me even touching it, revealing deep blackness beyond it—a dead space, void of any light or sound. The room pulls me in and swallows me, and for a moment or two I'm without any bearings, my senses enveloped by the chasm.

This indeed recalls the feeling I had when I was nine years old, and floated above the floor of my basement— I just jumped up and hovered. For several decades, my adult brain has tamped down that strange event, passing it off as a mere child's dream.

A tiny pin of light shines ahead giving me the first perspective of a finite space. The light grows stronger, and I hear laughter echoing and bouncing as if there are walls very close around me. Judging by the sound, it's obvious that little by little, the space I'm encapsulated in is beginning to expand, for the laughter is getting softer and much less cacophonous.

More light begins to fill out my blackened vision, and I find I'm standing in quite a large room, one that most assuredly couldn't fit in a modestly sized Upper East Side apartment building. After my free-floating experience, the light and gravity feels burdensome and unnatural.

There is a desk, and a silhouetted figure of a man sitting at it writing something. My surroundings normalize giving me a chance to get a closer look at him. Once again, it's plain to see that this man is me—this time older and in poor spirits, engaged in writing a letter. It's the very letter that I'd received beckoning me to New York.

"Oh you silly boy," Mae scolds him coldly, though in a motherly way. "I turn my back on you for a few minutes and you write a rescue letter… as if it will ever get back to the valley."

Clearly, she didn't know I had already received it, which gave me some hope. She then turns towards me and I feel the Six Devils letter buzzing again.

"You see, Truman, it is not I who's behind all of this."

With a cold sweat breaking out all over my body, I look at it, and sure enough—it has saved the worst for last.

Number Six — You.

Staring at it, I start feeling very ill, but deep down I can honestly say I'm not very surprised. It's true; I have simply led a selfish, childish life, and I'm starting to realize that I've hurt more people with my behavior than I'd ever thought possible.

I'm really not too different from all the people that I hate in Hollywood; I was only into myself, my feelings, my sadness or happiness, my success or failures. It's been all about me for quite some time, and now I was going be damned for it.

"What do you think of hell, Truman?" Her words are cold, and I wondered if I was already dead. "Does this match your mortal's estimation of what it would be? Probably not, everyone's always surprised. But then again, no two hells are the same for any two people. This is yours son—well, you could spend many more happy years on earth if you'd just get your butt in gear and follow some orders.

"Truman, you were handpicked way before you ever came out West; I was merely assigned to guide you through. You had so much promise, we thought you'd be in Fischer's shoes in just a few years. Unlike you, he was smart and listened. Yes, I played a role in getting him to the top—not that he was very appreciative. You certainly did him in, didn't you?"

Her eyes widened with an excitable giddiness at the horror of murder.

"Yes, you're staring at yourself, Truman—this is you about five years from now, but you know there are six or seven of you in this room right now. All of your *yous* are here, you may not see them, but they're here, all of your sinners, all your bastards, all the womanizers and human beasts that you carried within you... problem is the goody-two-shoes you've become is also here."

The last sentence trails off in energy, pointing her old lumpy over-painted fingernail at me. Then, the older me that's writing the letter, lifts his head and looks up.

"It is not too late," my image stammers, but Mae interrupts.

"He's right if you play ball with us and fulfill your promise, you won't end up here in five years, a complete loser, you'll get everything that you want. So let me ask you, Truman, when was the last time anyone threatened you with getting everything you've ever wanted?"

"Don't believe her," my older image says. "This is your destiny now or later, eventually you'll fall out of favor and end up here... you know it's true."

"He is only miserable like this because you're rebelling," Mae says. She then turns towards my weaker self. "How you escaped the valley is anyone's guess. You pathetic piece of crap."

This time I am not armed with a .45 or a revolver, but have a weapon of a different sort. I try to remain as cool as I can in order to pull it off.

"Why don't you let him be and concentrate on me, Mae? I have something to show you."

I take out the envelope from my pocket and finally obeying Sherry's instructions, hand them to their intended recipient. Inside there are ten photographs of two children—two beautiful blonde haired children, a girl and a boy.

"What do you have there, Truman?"

"Well let's see, Mae, it says on the back of these

photographs, *McLaughlin Grandkids*—I guess that'd make them your grandkids."

Mae leaves the side of my tortured self and comes around the desk with a very mistrusting though inquisitive face. There's a definitive crack in her menace.

"I don't have any grandkids. My son John never had any children."

"He had them four years ago, according to the ages and dates on these photos Mae."

"I left only two years ago, he would have told me that I had grandkids... he would have said something."

"If I remember correctly, Mae, you stopped talking to your son. He was a 'blue-collar Orange-County loser' as you used to call him—at least that's what you called him when you were at your Mai-Tai best."

The fact that Sherry had these photographs now makes sense, I remember her telling me that she knew Mae's daughter in law—they were both in acting class together.

Mae grabs the photos from my hands and turns away to look at them.

"You think you can fool me with these photos, you think I believe you about these... grandkids?" Her eyes take on an almost human look to them. She stares at the photographs of the beautiful little children.

"Yes, Mae," I tell her softly. "Those are your grandkids."

She brings them close to her face as if she were going to eat the photos. My tortured older self sees that she's distracted by them and looks at me for the first time with recognizable human emotion in his face.

"I have something to tell you," I say to him.

Mae is distracted by the photos and drops her guard, so I move closer to my older self and say the words that I heard many years ago as a small boy.

"Your name is Truman Morrow—remember what Dad said, 'No one is any less or better than you.' Truman, don't take any crap from this bitch."

Hearing the words he needed to hear, my image begins to stand and hands me the letter, the one that I have already received.

Then I tell him, "I release us."

Mae becomes distraught as she looks at each picture over and over, shuffling them faster and faster, just like playing cards. She starts trembling and begins to look very frail. The room also begins to shake as the rim around my vision distorts—as the shaking becomes severe, my older image seizes the opportunity to get up out of his chair and head for the door.

"See you in the valley," he says.

Mae's holds the photos of her grandchildren and violently screams at my image to stop. He slowly walks out into the lobby as the room begins to fade to deep darkness once more. He shuts the door behind him, and with a jarring reversal, the room immediately fills with a flash of blinding light.

The light is a garish opposite to the dark gloomy New York apartment, and it becomes apparent that I am now standing in a completely different space. As my eyes adjust to the light I see that Mae and I are indeed somewhere else; for we are now standing where we stood when I first saw her apparition—on the corner of Lankershim Boulevard in the good old San Fernando Valley.

The shaking continues, and it's obvious that it's an earthquake, probably a decent 5.0 on the Richter scale by the feel of it. As the shaking subsides, I look at Mae and she still is holding the pictures, but now with tears streaming down her face.

"Years ago, I was given a choice. The simple poor life, or the prosperous powerful one—damn, I gave up so very much, so very, very much. I have an existence now, but it lives only to feed in pure darkness," she pauses to look up at me, her hands shaking still. "Look at these babies," she sobs, "look at how beautiful they are. This boy looks like my brother, and this baby girl looks just like me when I was her age. Truman, look at all I've missed. Look at these babies—my babies."

Even with all the heartache she'd caused, and with all the destruction she was responsible for, I still feel so bad for her. Mae is completely and utterly pathetic at this moment, finally realizing what she's given up in life. I know Sherry would pity this woman, and take no joy in the poetic justice that is now being metered out by her from beyond the grave.

I hear the familiar whirring drone, and know even without looking, that a mattress pickup truck had driven up behind me. However, I keep my eyes fixed on Mae, for my job isn't finished.

"Go visit them for me, Truman. Tell them funny stories about their Grandma."

She smiles through very human tears as she holds the photos close to her breast then begins to walk out into the empty boulevard, shuffling in small energy-less steps. She turns back to look at me, and her appearance is now one of a corpse.

In seconds, her face and body rapidly decay as if the years since her death have come rushing to catch up with her. She turns back again and continues into the street, nearly a skeleton, skin falling off her body to the street below. She gives me a final beckoning look, and I knew what she wanted.

"Mae—I release you," I tell her.

What's left of her face smiles, and with that, the present hold on time is lifted, and Lankershim Boulevard becomes a roaring careless thoroughfare in the hot valley sun once again.

She is about midway out into the first lane when present time returns and the passing cars viciously eviscerate her, leaving nothing but a dusty smoke where she stood. Clearly, when the cars plowed her down, they saw nothing, and most likely didn't even notice the photographs flying up into the air. No one stopped or even slowed down.

I check the date on my cell phone, and for a brief moment it's June 1, and then suddenly it changes to

October 1, and with that, the whirring drone of the mattress truck stops. I look over to where the truck should be but see my 1964 Dodge instead, just as it was when this all started. For years, I've questioned but never realized why I was always seeing those mattress pickup trucks. Now I know——they were busy watching me.

I guess the San Fernando Valley will always survive—that is of course until the real big one hits, and it becomes a sea once more. The valley's been through many changes, with the only two constants being the sunshine, and the perpetual struggle to protect the what's left of the beloved land of Fathers Serra and Crespi.

It's just the age old struggle between good and evil, and if you are questioning the validity of those polarizing choices, or seeking their equivalence, then you will most likely fail when you're called to distinguish between them.

CHAPTER 20
THE VENERABLE WOMEN

AGING FOR THE immature can be a painful thing; our bodies grow old and tired, while our minds stay lost in youth. This episode in my life has served as a delayed maturation of sorts. I've been tempered and tested with the deepest horror and the finest love. I've been to hell, heaven, and back here to the strangest space of all; our human space that splits the infinite. (Yes, Roberto, I finally get it.)

I see it all very clearly now; Serra, Crespi and his California Mission protected the valley for a while. They knew about the devils, chased them down, capped their portals and beamed down God through the missions. Over the years, the amount of fighters dwindled, mainly because more and more people believed there wasn't ever anything to fight about.

Eventually, in modern times, "It's all good" became the mantra of the moral equivalists leaving this valley without any sentries and its gates to hell unguarded.

Evil boomed in the valley, where it's continued to grow almost uninhibited to such a sophisticated state that we don't even recognize it anymore. It's just everyday life to us, and we say things like, "It is what it is" and "whatever" in dismissal of what we truly know is dark and wrong. So now, only the Mattress Men are bearing the responsibility of watching it all. The studio gates still present a problem—too many fiends are able to hide behind them and work their destruction from within.

The next day after a long rest, I stroll the lonely streets of North Hollywood sadly coming upon the now closed shop where Jane's place should be. I'm not very surprised for the store has obviously been empty for years. The calendar on the wall is about three years old, and long forgotten sun-faded junk mail is strewn about the entry. No furniture, no record bins, no beautiful Jane.

The long since faded note on the dusty desk that was written by the previous owner, Trader John, is in plain sight and simply reads: *Out of Business.*

Taped to the window on the outside is a recent handwritten note.

> *Their apostolic labors of Father Serra and his*
> *party having been finished, they were upon their*
> *way back, and at the end of a few days journey,*
> *when the sun was about to set, they knew not*

*where to spend the night, and considered it certain
that they must sleep upon the plain.*

*They were thinking about this when they saw
near the road a house; whither they went and
solicited lodging. They found a venerable man,
with his wife and child, who received them with
much kindness and attention, and gave them
supper.*

*In the morning, the Fathers thanked their
hosts, and taking leave, pursued their way. After
having gone a little distance they met some
muleteers, who asked them where they had passed
the night. When the place was described, the
muleteers declared that there was no such house
or ranche near the road, or within many leagues.*
(2)

I knew all at once, that if I went over to Jane's
apartment on Otswego Street, I'd find someone else at
home—someone without the candles, the record player,
or the charm. I couldn't bear that.

As I turn to back walk home, a pickup truck piled
high with six mattresses rolls past. If this were a movie,
I would raise my hand in salute and wait for the fade to
black. I calmly recognize the two beautiful women sitting in the front bench seat of the truck. Roberto is driving and nods his head to me.

A gust of hot valley wind blows some garbage and
gritty Santa Ana sand to my feet, driving home the ugly

point of how real and sad this moment is. I'm too tired and dejected to raise my hand, but as the Mattress Man and his two beautiful passengers drive by, something from the top of the mattresses blows off the truck and lands in front of me.

The lovely old photograph of the beautiful woman in a rose garden, the one from sweet Jane's record store, shines up at me. I could have sworn that when I last saw this photograph, it was black and white. Now in color, there are two women, and where it previously read *Come to Lankershim*, it now so very sadly reads:

With Love from Erica and Sherry — North Hollywood.

* * *

Truman Morrow and Detective Vega will return, this time in our nation's capital, in book two of the series:

SIX DEVILS ON THE ELLIPSE

* * *

32317130R00143

Made in the USA
Charleston, SC
14 August 2014